Praise f

A St

controlled and subtly crafted novel that deals with a deep
th of human experience: flawed love that is yet worth
uggling to preserve.'   Barry Unsworth

)ne of the best novels I have read for a long time… All
e best aspects of the English literary tradition are brought
,gether here and woven into a bright whole… destined to
come a kind of a classic.'   Alma Hromic, *Cape Argus*

:ake's voice is individual, lucid, moving.'
                    Madeleine Keane, *Image Magazine*

Son to the Father

mystical vision of ordinary life… brilliant and rapturous.'
                    Hugh Barnes, *Glasgow Herald*

novel of constraint and reflection… loaded with wit,
tertaining double meanings and cultural asides.'
ouglas Reid Skinner, *The Star and SA Times International*

eake) writes with dry ease on the difficulty of being alive.'
                    David Hughes, *Mail on Sunday*

Derek Jarman

ake's extraordinary achievement is to have captured the
rit of each age, tracking the growth of Jarman the artist
l man in the context of the changing world around him…
:ry great life is made greater by a great Life, and Peake has
en Derek Jarman the biography he deserves.'
                    Simon Edge, *Gay Times*

TONY PEAKE

NORTH FACING

First published in 2017 by
Myriad Editions
www.myriadeditions.com

Registered address:
Myriad Editions
New Internationalist, The Old Music Hall,
106–108 Cowley Rd, Oxford OX4 1JE

First printing
1 3 5 7 9 10 8 6 4 2

A CIP catalogue record for this book
is available from the British Library

ISBN (pbk): 978-0-9955900-2-1
ISBN (ebk): 978-0-9955900-3-8

Designed and typeset in Palatino
by WatchWord Editorial Services, London

Printed and bound in Great Britain
by Clays Ltd, St Ives plc

For my children and my grandchildren –
they are the future

'As a child you can't really comprehend the meaning of far-off events; you live more like an animal, in the present world of the senses and within the dimly perceived horizons set by adults.'

Justin Cartwright, *The Song Before It Is Sung*

'I have lived elsewhere all my life.'

C. J. Driver, 'Elsewhere'

One

STICKS AND STONES, Paul's mother would say, *may break your bones, but words will never hurt you.*

Remembering, I have only to close my eyes and there he is, my childhood self, pleading before another.

'But this term you said to try again! I might get lucky. That's what you said. You practically promised!'

It's 1962. Wednesday, October 3rd, 1962, to be precise, in the playground of a private boarding school in Pretoria.

'*Might*,' said the other. 'I said *might*. I promised nothing.'

'But that isn't fair!'

'Come again?'

'What you're doing, du Toit. It isn't fair.'

'And who are you – hey, Harvey, of all people? – to tell an *ou* what is and isn't fair?'

'Saying no to me now when only last term—'

'Stupid *sout-piel.*'

He had with him some of his club: Strover; Labuschagne; Slug, of course. Who instantly provided the gleeful chorus: '*Sout-piel! Sout-piel!*' Someone with one foot in England, the other in South Africa, a penis that dangles, undecided, in the sea. *Salt cock* would be the slang's exact translation from the Afrikaans.

'Just because my parents were born … ' began Paul, though no sooner had he started along this line of defence than he realised its futility. Even supposing he found the right combination of words – words, again! – his adversaries still possessed a stronger one. So he just retreated, as he invariably did before du Toit and his cohorts, to lick his figurative wounds – the sort that only words can cause – elsewhere.

The playground of the school attended by Paul and du Toit, Strover and Labuschagne and the so-called Slug – along with over a hundred other boys, all presently milling about – was an area of ochre earth lying between the main building with its attached line of red-brick classrooms, and the cool green of the playing fields beyond, which was where Paul now headed because, since the fields were out of bounds during break, there he could temporarily escape du Toit's relentless teasing.

It had all started in their second year, when Paul had been rash enough to take into school one of his most treasured possessions: a diary given him by his maternal grandmother. The one who'd also suggested, at around the same time, that he be sent to live with her in England after what had happened in a place called Sharpeville. It was a five-year diary and had come wrapped in layers of rustling tissue paper. Just as soft, and wonderfully smooth, was its white leather cover. Though best of all for Paul was that it boasted a brass lock and a miniature key. He could write there what he would never dare write anywhere else.

But then the diary had somehow, sickeningly, vanished from his locker, resulting in such panicked misery that, even now, the mere thought of it could make his whole body prickle. The thought that by his own foolishness – for it had been foolish, incredibly foolish, to bring the diary into school, he saw that now – he'd made himself so vulnerable.

Stupid, stupid, stupid!

And how on earth was he to get it back? That was the next thing. He hadn't the remotest idea, and it was only at the end of a long, nerve-racked week – on the Saturday before lights-out – that Bentley major, in the bed alongside his, had put a stop to Paul's covert nightly sobbing by naming du Toit as the culprit. Though yet more tears had needed to be shed before du Toit had eventually got his right-hand man, Lombard, to fetch the diary, which he'd then carelessly tossed, along with its little key, on to Paul's bed, saying he'd not found it interesting enough to keep.

That was when the teasing had started.

Sissy! Mommy's boy! Coward!

And another Afrikaans taunt: *Rooi-nek!*

Because naturally the tanned du Toit didn't have anything as shaming as a red neck (unlike the pathetically pale Paul, whose mother kept him, as far as was humanly possible, out of the sun). Inescapable du Toit, who was also founder and captain of the school's most desired grouping. His own private club, uniquely configured. With other school gangs, the criteria for membership tended to be imprecise. In order to join du Toit's club, however, consisting as it did of just half a dozen specially chosen friends – ranked, it was said, from one to six – in order to join this club and be assigned a ranking, rumour had it that each potential friend must first perform an introductory task. And then, so as to keep – or improve – his ranking within the club, any number of further tasks, all set by du Toit. Even if, like Lombard, you were number one, you still had to prove yourself. If you didn't, you could very quickly drop down the ranks and face expulsion.

Not easy, then, or straightforward, being a friend of du Toit's. A more sensible boy might have considered himself better off on the outside. But that would have been to ignore the added pressure of Paul's parents. Their always desiring the best for him. Desiring also for him to make them proud; they were constantly going on about that, too. Forever urging him to fit in at school. To make more friends, why didn't he? To belong. They didn't like to think of him as being so lonely, not when they were spending good money on his schooling. Couldn't he try harder? As a favour both to them *and* to himself.

Then news that du Toit's club had recently welcomed an unexpected new member – Slug, ridiculous Slug! – causing something in Paul to snap. If Slug could be invited to join, then surely he could too? Never mind

One

'Harvey, of all people' – what about 'Slug, of all people'? Slug who, as his nickname implied, was basically sub-human. Sub-human and repulsive. Fatter, for a start, than anyone else in their class. Short-sighted, too. Bottle-thick spectacles and body parts that wobbled as he walked, like pinkish jelly. But still a friend of du Toit's. The newest recruit. One of the élite.

Personal outrage, parental pressure: it was a potent mix and had, towards the end of last term, catapulted Paul into demanding of du Toit why he couldn't also become a friend. If Slug now was?

It was just before supper, when briefly there was no requirement to be anywhere specific. Except that you were not meant to be in the dormitory. Only after prep were you allowed to return there. Yet this was nevertheless where, in the end, Paul had found du Toit, lying nonchalantly on his bed in a blaze of sunlight.

Their dormitory had once been an upstairs stoep or veranda and, as a result, was largely open to the outside world. Three canvas blinds, now furled, were all that protected it from the elements, hence the copious sunlight flooding the neatly made beds, six of which stood below the open blinds, six against the opposite wall, each separated from its neighbours by a curtained locker, the one place in school (apart from your desk, which was meant only for classroom use) where you could keep items of a personal nature. Bentley major, his recently removed appendix in a bottle. Strover, his collection of signed photographs of the country's cricketers. And Paul – for a bit – his diary. Which was maybe how du Toit had come across it? From being alone in the dormitory when he shouldn't have been.

This thought, and the memories it triggered of that agonising week, had encouraged Paul to meet du Toit's gaze head-on and say, 'I'd be better than Slug for a start. Slug's ugly and really clumsy at things.'

'So! Harvey wants to do things for me! That's tit.'

'I just want to know why you think I can't be a friend. We're in the same class, aren't we? The same dormitory. We're both in Spier's General Knowledge Club.'

'What's Spier got to do with it?'

'I'm not so different,' continued Paul breathlessly, 'is what I'm saying. Even though you think I am. *And* I'm never horrid to you.' This, for him, was the clincher. 'So why are you always so horrid to *me*?'

Du Toit smiled. Sharp white teeth in a gilded face. Teeth that distracted Paul from noticing the look of faint speculation in the cool blue eyes.

'Okay,' he said, sitting up. 'Ask again next term. You might get lucky next term.'

Then the bell had rung for supper, bringing the encounter to an end. And now another bell was ringing too, signalling another closure: of morning break, of Paul's false hopes. For, all through the holidays, he'd imagined that in the new term du Toit would be true to his word. He'd be set a task, he'd perform it and hey presto! No more *sout-piel*. No more *rooi-nek*.

It was all so unfair! He'd used the right word, in challenging du Toit. 'Unfair, unfair, unfair!' he repeated aloud, kicking at the edge of the playing field, since in his present state it was an equal insult that grass should be allowed to lord it over bare earth.

Then he froze. In the middle distance, the green sweep of the field framed the dark outline of a crouching figure: Pheko, the school groundsman, rewhitening the lines on the pitch in anticipation of that Saturday's inter-school cricket match. Were Pheko to see him kicking his precious field, he'd surely remonstrate. As might another figure Paul also clocked in the middle distance, striding towards the compound where the live-in masters had their bungalows.

There were two such compounds on the edge of the school grounds: a hedged one for staff, out of bounds to boys unless you were invited in – like, say, for Spier's General Knowledge Club – and a smaller, walled grouping of much plainer dwellings, more hut than bungalow, near the ditch where du Toit also had a hut, the one where his own club meetings were held. Here was where the school labourers lived: Pheko and two other men whose names Paul didn't know, plus an indeterminate number of uniformed women who made the beds, swept the corridors, cooked the meals and served at table. Also nameless.

Though Paul could of course easily name the figure striding into the distance: Spier, whose history class came next and already the bell had rung, so why wasn't the master hurrying *towards* the classrooms?

Odd, that.

Pressing the back of a bony wrist into each eye in case of telltale tears, Paul started back across the bare red earth of the playground. Past the thatched rondavel at its centre, home to the tuck shop, and past the whitewashed arch nearby, from which hung the school bell. Heading for the line of brick-built classrooms, as red in colour as the playground itself, before which stood a quartet of implacable boys, providers of the gleeful chorus:

'*Sout-piel! Sout-piel!*'

Two

I'VE STOPPED to pee and so notice, in the dust at my feet, a coincidental scattering of stones, most the colour of dried blood, bracketed by some whitened sticks. Mum's phrase given roadside substance.

Sticks and stones...

Really, Mum?

Zipping up, I aim a closet kick at the nearest stick, one that appears more bone than wood, that's how bleached it's been by the sun. Then I hear an approaching car: the dusty Ford I've been distantly, intermittently aware of in my rear-view mirror.

It slows and I see its three occupants. They see me too, their blatant regard making me feel, as they glide by, that I'm being sized up. Older white man alone on the roadside, having just relieved himself. I'm familiar with the stories. Ambushes. Hijacks. People killed for the money in their wallet, their laptops, their clothes, their hire car. The astounding cheapness of human life in South Africa. And the vanishing car *is* old; poorly maintained, too. Never mind the colour of their skin.

I jump into my own car and turn the ignition. Oh, I'm back all right – in spades! Though, when it comes to being ambushed, what should I fear more? The present? Or the past?

I reach for the brake and, with it, another question. Can I really help the ghosts of that past, childhood self included, achieve peace, release, on the basis of one impulsive trip? Or – just as that trio might be doing, up ahead – will my ghosts continue to lie in wait for me? Continue to torment?

It doesn't bear thinking about and so I try instead to concentrate on the present, each half-remembered tree and sun-burnished rock of it, now that Gauteng is behind me. The limitless sky. The dead-straight, if potholed road. That sense the country can often grant, of opportunity. Of opening up before you. Like treasure.

Until, that is, the sun starts to set, coalescing from fiery glare into a simplified red disc that slips, inch by steady inch, below the far horizon, carrying me back to a series of earlier October sunsets, which a twelve-year-old called Paul – Harvey, to his peers – had once scanned for signs that the world might be about to end.

St Luke's wasn't large: being privately run, it favoured exclusivity over size, a luxury denied its government counterparts. Yet, to a child, the main building none-theless seemed substantial. Would it still? I wonder. You approached it via a circular drive where parents might park when dropping off or collecting their charges. There was a suggestion of lawn here, too, and some flowerbeds: Pheko's domain. Then the bougainvillea-draped façade of a two-storeyed, rather old-fashioned brick building whose red steps led up to a double door of dark wood which, in turn, opened on to a corridor that ran the entire length of the building before leading you outside again, via a further set of steps that descended into the playground. Off this corridor, to the right, was the hall where assembly was held, meals taken and, once a term or so, plays staged and film shows arranged. To the left lay the headmaster's study, the library, the sick-bay, the downstairs toilets and the kitchens. While upstairs, of course, were the dormitories – five in all – and showers and further toilets.

What am I forgetting?

The classrooms – again, five in all – are already accounted for, as are the tuck shop and nearby bell, whose function it was to regulate the day. But I realise I've left out the swimming pool to the other side of the main building from the classrooms; that and the wooden sports pavilion, focal point of the playing fields.

Anything else?

I home in on the hedged compound on the far side of the fields, where the live-in masters had their bungalows. There were four of these, each built of the same red brick as the classrooms, each roofed in green corrugated iron while their metal windows and wooden doors were painted purple, the school colour; all set around a small square of lawn, on which some toys happen to be lying. Two dolls and a scattering of miniature tea things: cups and saucers, a milk jug, a teapot. Stanford – one of the married masters – had two young daughters, clearly keen on playing house.

But I'm not in search of Stanford. It's the unmarried Spier I want and so it's through *his* purple door that my memory now speeds.

Although externally Spier's bungalow was identical to the other three, internally it told another story; at least, his study did. His desk, for instance, was vastly more untidy than Stanford's, or even old MacWilliam's. It was also devoid of family photos. Nor were the books on his shelves all serious-looking hardbacks; he had just as many paperbacks, some with quite lurid covers, which he didn't mind you taking down and looking at. In fact, he encouraged it and there was, on his untidy desk, a small black book for keeping track of what he'd loaned to whom.

His *anti-library*, he called it.

In addition, he wore his haphazardly combed, rich brown hair a good deal longer than the other, generally older-seeming masters. He seldom donned a tie or jacket. He rolled up his shirt sleeves and often had ink stains on his shirt fronts.

In short, he stood apart from his fellow teachers and, as a consequence, was thrilling to be with. If Paul had known the word, he might even have said Spier was subversive. But *subversive* wasn't in Paul's lexicon. Not yet.

'*TWO DIE, SCORES INJURED*,' Spier was saying, reading from that Monday's paper to the six boys sitting before him, '*AS NEGRO-HATING WHITES RIOT IN AMERICA.*'

He looked up from where he was perched, alongside a teetering pile of exercise books, on the edge of his disordered desk. 'So what's the background here?' he demanded. 'Who is James Meredith? Anyone?'

The General Knowledge Club met weekly, before supper on Thursdays, its hand-picked members being: Bentley major, Lombard, Horton, Strover, du Toit and Paul. An improbable grouping, though Paul had never thought to question why Spier had made the choices that he had. He was just happy to take at face value the fact that – for once! at last! – he'd been included. Even when, like now, he didn't know the answer to Spier's question.

'No one? Really? Horton?'

Horton, mouth ajar as usual – some said because he enjoyed revolting people with his saliva-strung braces – just shifted in his seat; and then, lest Spier think for a moment that he did have anything to contribute, decisively shut his gaping mouth.

'Strover?'

But Strover would only have read – if anything – the sports pages.

The pair most likely to answer Spier's question were Bentley major and Lombard. Lombard because he was the brightest pupil in their class; Bentley major because he was both a class *and* a dormitory monitor. However, before Spier could turn to either of them, du Toit, who was sitting next to Paul, diverted the master's attention by trying to slip Paul a scrap of paper on which he'd scribbled something.

'Ah, du Toit!' said Spier, with a darting smile. 'I knew you wouldn't let me down. Still, rather than trying to pass the answer to Harvey, why don't you enlighten us yourself? Please, be my guest!'

'I'm sorry, sir,' said du Toit, surreptitiously pocketing his scrap of paper, 'but it was Harvey who was trying to tell *me* something, so I wasn't really listening. My fault, sir. I'm sorry.'

'Heavens, Harvey!' said Spier, smoothly transferring his smiling attention to Paul. 'That's too bad when, as we all know, du Toit here struggles to concentrate on things that don't immediately concern him. You should show more consideration.'

Then, before anything further could be said, or implied, Lombard produced what Spier was after.

'Sir, hasn't he upset everyone because they don't actually want him at their university? Isn't that what the fuss is all about?'

'At last!' crowed Spier. 'Though why do you say "their" university? And people have died, hey, Lombard. "Fuss" is perhaps too gentle a word. *Ja*, Bentley? You've been rather quiet this afternoon. Nothing to add?'

'Well, sir, the university's in what they call the Deep South,' proffered the monitor. 'Mississippi, I think.'

And so they were off, no longer bound by the book-lined walls of Spier's study, but at large in the outside world, a favourite phrase of Spier's, who believed that only by transporting yourself in this way could you hope to understand home. Precisely the point, he liked to say, of general knowledge. The outside world. What you learned there to bring back. Though he didn't always make the connections clear, preferring instead to have the club join the dots for themselves.

'Right!' he went on, settling more securely on his desk, an action which fleetingly delineated, within their casing of grey flannel, the muscularity of his thighs. 'At the University of Mississippi recently, a black student by the name of James Meredith registered to study. Why is this news-worthy? Because, in the Deep South, they practise segregation. What we term apartheid. With me so far?'

Six heads nodded in dutiful unison.

'And our James Meredith,' continued Spier, 'having brought a case earlier – successfully, too – against central government, questioning their right to stop him going to any university he wants, enrols in one where the attitude of the whites – being Southerners, Mississippians believe in segregation, most of them – has meant he's had to be escorted on to campus under guard. The inevitable protests then became a riot, troops had to be called and so we get our headline.' Holding up the paper he'd quoted from earlier, he opened it to an inside page.

'We also get: *Americans are bitter about the attempts of the Communists, particularly Moscow, to exploit the situation. Mississippi, they feel, has given the outside world a wrong impression of the vast strides made by the government and people of the country in resolving colour problems, particularly in the South. The Americans at the United Nations...*' Here Spier glanced up. 'Remember,' he said, 'we talked about the United Nations last time? *The Americans at the United Nations also believe that the firm and resolute action taken by President Kennedy to uphold the law which provides for desegregation throughout the land will show the Russians that the United States can be equally determined and resolute in dealing with international problems such as Berlin, Cuba, and other East-West difficulties.*'

That must have been the first time Cuba was mentioned, though, since it was in such a baffling article, no one noticed. Paul wondered if any of the others had understood the piece better. Or picked up, as he had, on its use of the phrase 'outside world'.

At the far end of the semi-circle of chairs ranged before Spier's desk sat freckled, red-haired Horton, mouth open again, moist braces on show. Next came stocky, sports-mad Strover with his air of unconscious belligerence – unconscious because he was, in fact, generally unbelligerent by nature, placid, even; in bovine terms, a ruminative cow rather than a raging bull. Then the keen, bespectacled form of Lombard, who appeared as if he might be grasping things. Then the baleful presence of neighbouring du Toit, whom Paul avoided looking at;

and, on Paul's left, the quiet yet watchful Bentley major, who was the next to say something.

'So who, sir, is breaking the law?' he asked. 'If they have one law in the Deep South, but central government says differently, who is actually right, sir?'

Surprisingly, Strover had a view on this. 'The government, silly.'

Lombard, however, wasn't so sure. 'But if you do things differently in your own state,' he put in, 'then wouldn't you be breaking your own laws if you only listened to central government?'

'Is there not a moral dimension here?' probed Spier. 'Some higher law?'

'Well, sir,' said du Toit, always a late contributor to their discussions, 'there's human nature. People all over the world, Pa says, want to stick to their own kind, and it always makes for trouble, he says, bad trouble sometimes, when people forget.'

'Goodness!' said Spier, who by this stage had quit his desk and was pacing the room. 'So you're telling me that your father —'

But here he was interrupted by Strover. 'Sir, can we please just talk about the fight for a bit? *Ag*, can we, sir? Please!' He meant of course the boxing match between Sonny Liston and Floyd Patterson, something else to have come out of America recently. Something, too, that had been exercising Strover greatly. Why had it been so one-sided? And what about that first round knock-out! Said to be the third fastest ever in a world heavyweight title fight. Unbelievable, no?

Then Lombard intervened, as he frequently did, with a knock-out all his own.

'Sir! Have you seen the time? Supper in ten minutes.'

Spier consulted his own watch before moving towards the door. 'Right!' he said. 'Vamoose! And please: more of an effort this weekend in reading the papers.' He stood aside from the opened door to let them pass. 'Okay?'

Usually du Toit led the exit charge, and with such alacrity that you'd be forgiven for thinking a fire had broken out, rather than their facing the prospect of, say, baked beans on tepid toast, glasses of milk and, if they were lucky, a pudding. Frogs' eggs, maybe, as tapioca was called. But today du Toit held back and it was Bentley major, uncombed hair sticking up at the back, who exited first. Then Horton; strutting Strover; Lombard; then Paul.

'You look pensive, Harvey,' said Spier. 'Everything all right?'

'What, sir? Sorry, sir!' said Paul.

'Sad, even,' mused the master, fixing him with the brownest of brown eyes. 'Are we?'

'Sir?'

Sotto voce, Spier – who'd put out a hand to draw the passing Paul closer – added, 'Stand your ground, boy. Be your own man. And as for you, du Toit,' since du Toit had by now entered the frame, 'if you're going to pass notes in my presence, try to do it without me seeing.'

'Note, sir?' said du Toit, affecting bewilderment. 'What note?'

'The one intended for Harvey,' said Spier. 'Still in your pocket, I presume.'

'Pocket, sir?'

Spier's hand shot out again, causing Paul to notice anew how the hairs on the back of it ran in a diagonal line from just above the thumb to above the little finger. Lushly, as on Spier's bare forearms. 'Hand it over.'

'But sir...'

'Chop-chop, du Toit, unless you want to be late for supper too.'

Du Toit hesitated, but only fractionally.

'*Die rooi gevaar*,' said Spier thoughtfully, perusing what he'd been handed. 'Well, well! So you were listening the other week, when we touched on the Cold War and the West's fear of all things red!' He looked towards Paul. 'Though why he wants *you* to ask me about the communists is beyond me. When he could just as easily, more easily, do it himself.' He returned his gaze to du Toit. 'Unless you're thinking we could get into trouble for talking about these things and you wanted Harvey here to cop it? Did you?'

'Sir?'

'Because if so, I'd like you to remember, please, that what we talk about in General Knowledge can always stay within these walls. Between ourselves. This note, du Toit...' he crumpled it into a little ball before lobbing it in the direction of his already full waste-paper basket '...is not only unpleasant, it's also unnecessary. Got that?'

'Yes, sir,' said du Toit. 'Sorry, sir.' Followed by, moments later, as together he and Paul skirted the dolls and miniature tea things lying out on the grass, 'Bloody Spier! Why do we have these stupid clubs?'

A question that in and of itself raised so many issues that Paul wouldn't have known how to begin answering it, even if the bell for supper hadn't then sounded, forcing the two of them into a risky dash across the forbidden middle of the playing fields.

They arrived, panting painfully, at the main building to find the plump form of their science master at the top of the steps, overseeing an orderly entry into supper. A separate line for each class.

'Cutting things a bit fine, aren't we?' Botma remarked as, still panting, du Toit and Paul filed past him. 'Lucky it's not Mr Stanford on duty, or it might have been detention.'

'Sorry, sir,' said Paul. 'We were...'

'Delayed by Mr Spier,' said du Toit, 'in General Knowledge.'

'Aha!' chuckled Botma. 'Knowledge! Yes, well, not for nothing do they call too much of it a dangerous thing.'

The table at which Paul sat for meals was also du Toit's, though, since the latter occupied a place near the head of it, Paul was always separated from his nemesis by the bulwark that was du Toit's club: Horton, Strover and Lombard from General Knowledge. Plus Labuschagne, Kintock and Slug, who weren't at all in Spier's circle. Which meant that after Botma had said grace – a few hastily intoned, barely comprehensible Latin phrases – there was little chance of discovering more about du Toit's mysterious note. Rather, it was business as usual as Paul's plate ran a familiar gauntlet from one club member's hand to another before finally reaching the table prefect who, despite not being a special friend of du Toit's, still contrived to dish Paul a little less than anyone else.

Or was he imagining that Eedes always did this? His mother would have said so. *And* his father. *Get a grip, old fruit.*

If only he could! Eyes pricked by the threat of yet more tears, Paul stared unhappily at his baked beans while all around him boys begged each other to pass the bread, the jam, not to guts the milk, to keep their elbows tucked in and what about that first round knock-out! Hey?

After supper came the lesser ordeal of prep, which also took place in the hall once the tables had been cleared by the army of uniformed women whose penultimate task of the day this was, their last being the washing-up. As a result, prep was underscored by a specific aural accompaniment: pens first, scratching on paper; then the percussive footsteps of the master on duty as he paced the hall – still Botma who, as the only master to smoke a pipe, which he kept, when not clamped between yellowing teeth, in the pocket of his jacket, stank as he passed you by; and finally, from across the corridor, a faint, essentially melodic counterpoint – the clink of crockery, the slushing of water, the 'music' made by the distant voices of the washers-up. The maids didn't sing as such as they went about their last task of the day; but their talk, being in a language foreign to Paul, nevertheless existed for him only in terms of its rise and fall, just like the notes of a song.

If du Toit had wanted to bother Paul now, he'd have had his work cut out. So it wasn't until after lights-out that the day delivered its *coup de grâce*.

It was unseasonably warm and the middle blind had been left open, allowing the star-speckled patch of sky opposite Paul's bed to absorb and disperse his worries. *Du Toit* and *Spier*. Not belonging properly. *Sout-piel*. *Rooi-nek*. *Rooi gevaar*. The prettiness of the stars out-twinkled mere words. *Sticks and stones*. Perhaps his mother was right.

Then, all at once, something, someone materialised by his bedside. A suggestion of sleek blond hair. Sharp white teeth.

Paul looked quickly sideways to see if Bentley major had noticed. But the monitor was asleep.

Stomach tightening, he twisted round again.

'What?' he hissed. 'What is it now? Here to call me more names? Or tell me again how pathetic you think my parents are? Just because they're English.'

The shadowy form didn't move. Nor, to start with, did it give anything away. If there was an expression in the eyes to indicate what the shadow was intending, Paul couldn't decipher it in the gloom. Only the halo of hair. That glint of teeth. A sense of urgency.

Then suddenly the face closed in on him, as if wanting, as his mother still did on occasion when tucking him up at night, to ... But how could that be? Du Toit of all people!

'What?' repeated Paul, voice all squeaky. 'Say it!'

Then a rushed whisper, like wind passing through loose grass, ending with, 'An ou's allowed to change his mind.'

Although the initial sequence of what had been said hadn't come out so clearly, Paul still grasped what was on offer. And by the club's captain too! When usually, or so he'd always been led to believe, it was du Toit's right-hand man whose task it was to invite new members in.

'Why?' he asked, voice squeakier still. 'Has something happened?'

'There's space,' murmured du Toit, pulling back at last, 'is all. And I already know, because you've already told me, how much you want it. No use pretending you don't.'

The shadowy face was back where it had been to start with, some feet away – although this didn't stop Paul's heart from continuing to race as the club captain quietly re-stated his surprise invitation against a backdrop of glittering stars.

'Well? Will you, or won't you, Harvey? Don't just lie there.'

Three

THERE ARE STARS in the present too, a whole windscreen full. Stars of such brilliance that, although there's no moon, still the landscape – flat and scrubby and dotted with small, stunted trees – is visible. Where the earth has coughed up rocks, they glimmer palely, like memories.

According to the Sat Nav, I've twenty kilometres to go before reaching my destination. About fifteen miles, then, in the course of which... well, there's still time for the Ford, under cover of darkness, to ambush me. Or has it merely turned off, heading for some settlement? I remember my father remarking once on the black people you saw when out driving, apparently walking from nowhere to nowhere across the vastness of the landscape. Never a village in sight.

'Do you ever wonder,' he'd said to my mother, sitting beside him, 'if they're paid by the government to do this?

Walk about in that fashion? As local colour? Part of the scenery?'

Whereas now, of course, the same people *are* more or less the government. A rainbow nation. Things have moved on. Or does the dusty Ford, whatever the intention of its occupants, suggest that the country is still, like me, too much hostage to the relentless, sapping power of the past?

'I don't understand it,' Paul's mother was saying. 'Mrs Merinkavitch manages and she hardly pays her garden any attention, just leaves it to her boy. Who, I might add, looks gormless.'

She was in her gardening clothes: a dun-coloured skirt long since demoted from best, a plain blouse, a pair of scuffed leather shoes with low heels, and, of course, owing to her mistrust of the sun, a wide-brimmed straw hat that obscured the fineness of her dark, wavy hair. In her gloved hand was a trowel.

'Back home,' she went on, 'Granny always used to say what green fingers I had. *This* climate, though…'

Grasping Paul's shoulder – for she'd been kneeling on a strip of sacking before the flowerbed in question – she used him to lever herself upright.

'In England you crave the sun. All the best houses are south-facing. Lack of rain is never an issue. Well, hardly. Things grow. And grow and grow. Willy-nilly. But here…' She let the trowel in her gloved hand fall against her skirt, smearing it with dust.

Paul lived with his parents in a small village that was generally regarded as being a cut above other such settlements on the fringes of Pretoria. Quarter-acre plots, common elsewhere, were non-existent in posh Nellmapius. In Nellmapius an acre was about the smallest you could get, with the result that trees were abundant; and, since greenery was, on the highveld, to be desired, so too was the village. Charming, people said. So different from its neighbours, so – well, English, they supposed. The sort of place where a person with Peggy's background might feel quite at home.

'It really is hopeless!' she concluded, gesturing with her trowel towards her wilting Transvaal daisies. 'Why do I even bother?'

Paul, wanting as ever to be supportive, replied brightly, 'But people always say how nice you've made the house. Everyone who visits, they all say that.'

It was an undistinguished building, the bungalow they inhabited; not at all desirable, or charming. Still, Paul was right. By dint of chintz and oak, Persian rugs, ornaments of a somewhat antique nature and pictures that often featured the English countryside, here Peggy had somehow contrived to hold her own. The house's only African aspect, apart from its architecture – the metal windows, the red tin roof – was Mosa, their maid.

Every morning, she'd emerge from behind the garage, where she occupied a room that smelled powerfully of paraffin and had in it, unlike the fussily furnished house, the barest minimum: just a chair, some hooks on

Three

the wall for her clothes and a single bed kept on bricks in order, as she'd once explained to a wide-eyed Paul, to deter an evil spirit called the *tokoloshe*, who liked, among other things, not specified, to bite off a sleeping person's toes. Your only defence against it was bricks because, being small, a *tokoloshe* couldn't, praise the lord, climb a brick.

From these cramped, smelly and potentially life-threatening quarters, Mosa would take up her early-morning station in the kitchen to brew the day's first pot of tea. This she would then carry, on a tray she'd laid the night before, to the master bedroom; although, now that Paul was boarding, during term-time, it was only on exeats that he still experienced the rhythms of life within the Harvey household.

On a Sunday, these were: his father, having collected Paul from school, would spend the morning in his workshop in the garage, while Peggy either tasked Mosa in the kitchen, or tended her hopeless garden. Then a substantial lunch at the oak table in the dining room, for even in high summer the Harveys never ate on the stoep, or braaied. Rather, they sat down at a formally laid table to a substantial roast, a medley of vegetables, a specially prepared pudding, all served by Mosa. Followed by a period of obligatory quiet, which Paul was required to spend in his room. Then tea in the lounge – which Peggy would serve herself, Mosa having by now been given 'off' – where Paul was made to eat so many sandwiches, always the sandwiches first, and so much cake – *We can't have you wasting away, dear!* – that, by the time he clambered into the car to be driven back to St Luke's by Douglas, the dread he habitually felt at having to leave the security of home for another week of school was intensified by indigestion to the point where his stomach would actually be aching. Sometimes he even thought he might throw up.

Though on the weekend after du Toit's extraordinary nocturnal invitation, life hadn't, in fact, been following its usual patterns. In keeping with the strangeness, the surprise, the shock of that invitation, anomalies abounded, starting with Saturday's game of cricket against KGPS; or King George Preparatory School, to give St Luke's brother establishment its full name. Because the match was being played at home, after morning lessons and lunch those seniors not in the team had to present themselves on the sidelines in support of their first eleven. Also gathered there were some parents, the fathers in shorts and T-shirts mainly, the mothers in equally casual summer dresses, enticing dashes of colour against the field's prevailing green. Barring one pale father, who stood out in a beige suit, and one pale mother, whose skirt reached down to her calves when every other dress on display was above the knee. Making Paul wish, as he ran towards his parents – the sight of them always caused him to break into a run – that they could have been different. Or rather, not quite *so* different. That was what he really wanted. For them to blend in.

'Hello, darling. My, you look hot!' said Peggy, planting her customary kiss on his sweaty forehead, something

Three

else he could have done without. 'Must you always run so, instead of walking?'

Douglas, thankfully, was less demonstrative. He only lifted a vague hand, being anyway in conversation with Spier.

'How was Monday's test?' continued Peggy. 'Had you done enough revision? I wasn't sure from last Sunday. And your tuck? Did I bake sufficient?'

Here a heavy hand laid unexpected claim to Paul's shoulder and he heard a deep voice saying, in a rumbling Afrikaans accent, 'You're Paul, right? I recognise you from Andre's description. Don't act surprised. He's told me all about you. Oh, yes.'

Paul looked up into a pair of cat-like eyes, greenly set in a sunburnt face.

'And what I'm wondering is: would you like to come out with Andre on tomorrow's exeat? Back to our place, I mean?'

Douglas and Spier had both fallen silent.

'I'm sorry, but I don't think I...' It was Peggy who broke the silence.

'Koos,' said the man, extending a beefy arm. 'Koos du Toit.' He turned to shake hands with Douglas too, nodding briefly, as he did so, at Spier. 'Afternoon, Spier,' he said, then cleared his throat. 'I don't mean to put your boy on the spot or anything, but he and my son are such good friends, or so Andre's been telling me, Mrs...Harvey, isn't it?'

'Please,' said Paul's mother, 'call me Peggy.'

'And I'm Douglas,' said Paul's father.

'Me you know,' said Spier.

'*Ag*, we all know you, Mr Spier,' said du Toit's father with a barked laugh. 'You pop up all over the place.' His eyes, however, stayed on Peggy. 'So – how about it?'

First du Toit at my bedside, Paul was thinking, *now this! What could it all mean?*

Peggy sounded taken aback too. 'That's very kind of you,' she was saying, a look Paul couldn't recall having seen before entering her usually judicious grey-green eyes, 'but I'm afraid that tomorrow we have plans.'

'We do?'

Peggy shot her husband a more familiar look. 'Honestly, Douglas! You must remember! Father Ashley – yes? – and Simon. Simon's coming too. I've shopped and everything.'

'Simon?' interjected Spier. 'You don't by any chance mean Simon Tindall, do you?'

'Why?' said Peggy. 'Do you know him?'

'A bit.'

'Like I say,' said Mr du Toit, 'our Mr Spier pops up everywhere. But, for those of us who haven't got a finger in every pie, you have to tell me, Peggy, please! Who are these *blerrie* people?'

Paul considered the figures encircling him. The untidiness of Spier, who had some bilious grass stains down one side of his poorly ironed shirt; the mildness of his father, all milky-blue eyes and gingery hair; his mother's – well, elegance, he supposed, even if she did wear her skirts too long, too severe; and, last but not least, Mr du Toit in his tightly fitting, short-sleeved, well-

30

pressed khaki shirt that matched his shorts, while on his feet were flip-flops, meaning that in his case the amount of flesh on show was positively indecent. At least Spier had longs on.

Peggy, meanwhile, one hand having come to rest on Paul's head – she'd drawn him close after Mr du Toit had touched his shoulder – was detailing why Paul couldn't accept Mr du Toit's invitation. Ever since a bout of malaria had carried off Father Ashley's wife, she explained, leaving him to cope alone with their only son, she and Douglas had liked, when possible, to lighten the vicar's Sundays. It was such a burdensome day for a priest and he gave so much to Nellmapius. Plus there was the fact that, since he came from England too, he'd absolutely no family in the country to help with Simon. Who was *such* a trial. As Mr Spier would know, presumably.

'Quite the rebel, then,' said Mr du Toit, 'for the son of a priest. Or the friend of a schoolmaster, even. How did you get to meet, Spier?'

'Oh, just through varsity.'

'But then losing one's mother,' Peggy went on, 'can never be easy.' The pressure of her hand on Paul's head intensified. 'So if Simon's a bit too political, perhaps it's only to be expected. And all the more reason, say I, to give poor Father Ashley lunch when we can. As a family.'

'Not forgetting,' added Douglas, 'how you do like someone to talk to about England. Don't you, dear?'

'Don't we both?'

'So, okay,' said Mr du Toit, raising his fair-sized arms in a fine display of defeat. 'I get the point. Mind my own business and no chance tomorrow for me. But please, I'd really like it if Paul could still come and visit. How about next Sunday? I could pick him up when I fetch Andre and then, afterwards, you could join us for a *lekker* lunch. I can't promise to talk about England, I've never been, but I can always show you a slice of the real South Africa. There've been du Toits in the Transvaal since before it was declared a republic the last time. A Boer republic. What do you say?'

'Well, Peggy?' queried Douglas. 'We're not having Father Ashley two Sundays running, are we?'

'My, my,' said Peggy. 'Goodness!' She'd lifted her hand from Paul's head to pat nervously at her own hair. 'This is so unexpected. What can I say?'

'*Yes*, I hope,' said Mr du Toit. 'Or are you already doing that? I'm never sure with you English.'

'Over!'

The umpire's call served not just to galvanise the fielders into a change of position; it also drew a line under the conversation. Both Spier and Mr du Toit melted away, while Peggy, thus reminded that there couldn't be too many more overs to go before half-time, hurried towards the pavilion to help with the tea.

And was about to hurry away again now, from her disappointing daisies.

'Heavens!' she was saying, looking at her watch. 'I must see how Mosa is doing, or lunch will be ruined. Be an angel, Paul, and put my gardening things back in the garage, would you? There's a dear.' She handed him her gloves and trowel, then said, 'That very sunburnt man

32

with the crew-cut. Mr du Toit. You were looking at him so oddly yesterday.'

'No, I wasn't!'

'And his son? You've never mentioned him before. Andre, was it? Or have I forgotten? How long exactly have you two been friends?' And, when he didn't reply, 'Because please, if you have a particular friend, you must, must tell us. We like to share these things. You mean the world to us, you know. Always have. Always will.'

She was interrupted by a call from the back door – Mosa, with a merciful, 'Madam, the chicken!'

'I knew it!' sighed Peggy. 'No rest for the wicked. And don't you dawdle either, dear. The sacking too, all right?'

But Paul, shaken as he was by the knowledge that, sooner or later, he must find a way of telling Peggy about du Toit, did momentarily dawdle. On the one hand he was dying to boast about becoming a club member. What better proof of fitting in, finally? Of achieving what she and Douglas had always wanted? Yet, on the other, he couldn't see Peggy – or Douglas, for that matter – especially Douglas – much liking the club rules. To belong only at the expense of someone else, and by having constantly to prove yourself: would that really count with them as acceptance?

He doubted it.

And there was another thing to doubt. Could du Toit, who'd only just appeared at his bedside, really have told his father they were such good friends? Already? On what basis? And why?

Feeling unpleasantly hot suddenly, and not just because of the sun, he scooped up Peggy's sacking and headed worriedly for the cool of the garage.

'Hello there! Come to check on the old man, have we, see what the hell he's up to in his funny little workshop?'

Douglas had once confided in Paul that, as a youngster, he'd dreamed of being an engineer, had gone into insurance only because his father hadn't been rich enough to send him to university. Which was why, at weekends, he would gravitate towards a side section of the garage that exactly matched the area where, to the rear of it, Mosa had her room. Here he liked to design and make gadgets for Peggy to use about the house. Or for Paul to play with – most recently a home-made racing car track, currently laid out in the body of the garage. There wasn't the space for it anywhere else. Though, since he wasn't exactly enamoured of its home-made look and how erratically it functioned, Paul didn't actually use the track much. Just as Peggy didn't always utilise the household gadgets she got given, many of which didn't work well either and would end up back in the garage too, forlornly gathering dust on a shelf.

There were a great many shelves in the garage work-shop, serried ranks of them above and around and behind the cluttered work-bench over which Douglas was presently hunched: shelves for tools, for nails and screws, for paint, for brushes, for string and sandpaper. Douglas never threw anything away, however rusty or worn or bent.

'Well, providing you can keep a secret,' he went on, smiling conspiratorially, 'it's a little something for your mother's birthday.' He released from the vice a length of tapered metal tubing which, while Paul put Peggy's gardening things back on the crowded shelves, he held aloft. 'For planting bulbs, see. I haven't fixed the handle on it yet, but you press it into the ground, it makes a hole, then you drop the bulb into the hole *et voilà*! Spring colour in the garden. Or that's the hope.' As he spoke, he was simultaneously scanning the bench for something else. 'Your mother tries so hard,' he said, milky-blue eyes darting this way and that, 'and has such terrible luck. So anything I can do horticulturally, as it were... Well, I like to play a part, that's all.' Replacing his handiwork in the vice with one hand, he laid the other on what he'd been looking for: a sneaky packet of cigarettes. For Douglas was supposed to have given up.

'Speaking of your mother,' he said next, through a haze of smoke, 'has she said anything about Mr du Toit? You know, the father we met yesterday at the match. Afrikaans fellow. With the crew-cut.'

Paul's stomach tightened; but, in the event, Douglas didn't draw breath.

'Because if she does,' he continued, '*when* she does, I want you to treat it with a pinch of salt. The thing about your mother is – well, as you know, she's never felt completely at home here. Particularly since we left the Commonwealth, became a republic. And then there was all that Sharpeville palaver, when your grandmother, if you remember, got it into her head that we should put you on a plane so you could go and live with her. Because it wasn't safe here any longer, she thought. Quite erroneously, of course – more to do with her own loneliness now that your grandfather is no longer with us. But anyway, be that as it may, it's as well to realise, old fruit, that your mother can be a tad – just a tad – prejudiced against people for being Afrikaans. And as South Africans, which is what we are now – *you* most certainly – that's not something we can afford. Is it? One must fit in.' He tapped the ash from his cigarette on to the concrete floor, then scuffed at it with his foot. 'It wasn't an easy decision, coming here, but we've made our beds, we've had to, and I want you to know that I'm really proud of you for becoming friends with this du Toit fellow. Andre, am I right? Next weekend will be good for us. All three of us. The whole darn shooting match.'

Paul supposed he should have been grateful that his father hadn't required him to be specific about du Toit. (Although Douglas did have a few questions, none of which Paul could answer: Was Mr du Toit only a farmer, or did he do other things as well? And Mrs du Toit? Why hadn't *she* been at cricket? Were there other children? How big was the farm?) Yet he still felt exposed. Ultimately, too little had been nailed down, that was the problem. Like what lay behind du Toit's bedside behaviour, for a start; and why, for instance, his father had said Peggy was prejudiced, when Paul knew perfectly well that she wished for him to fit in too.

Coupled with which thought, Peggy could be heard calling from the back door, 'Douglas! Paul! Our guests are here!'

'Better look lively,' said Douglas, dropping his cig-arette to the floor and, just as he had earlier with its ash, taking care to grind it into dust. 'We don't want to be accused of curtailing your mother's chat about overseas, do we, now? And don't let's say anything about what we've just been discussing. Okay?' Paul noticed that, as Douglas spoke, he was also making certain he'd slipped his cigarettes beneath a tangle of rope and used sandpaper, where they couldn't be seen.

The kitchen was steamy round the stove from the pots bubbling away on its hobs, while, at the sink, Mosa, elbow-deep in foam, was tackling some washing-up. She'd rolled up her sleeves and was wearing an apron so that later, when she came to serve, her uniform wouldn't appear damp.

'Where's the madam?' asked Douglas.

'Madam is in the lounge,' said Mosa, pausing in her task. 'There with Father Ashley.'

'Have you put out the drinks?'

'Yes, master, on the tray.'

'Ice?'

'In its bucket, master.'

She turned her attention to Paul.

'Does the young master want that he wash his hands with me?' she asked quietly as Douglas departed, a mischievous sparkle in her eyes, for Paul was supposed to wash his hands only in the bathroom at the other end of the house. 'I won't tell the madam, never.'

Crossing eagerly to the sink, Paul squeezed between it and Mosa's comfortable form, thereby allowing her plump black hands with their pinkish palms to plunge his own, much smaller, paler hands into the tickly foam.

'Dry here,' she said afterwards, offering him a corner of her apron. 'Quick now, or the madam will come. And your hair, you must to do this.' She smoothed its fly-away blondness. 'There! Master is now good.'

As he entered the lounge, Paul saw that Peggy had also been attending to appearances. She'd changed into her green dress, one of Paul's favourites, and her mouth was newly lipsticked. Only Douglas, already at the sideboard pouring drinks, hadn't bothered with how he looked. Though, since Douglas always wore an office shirt anyway, and trousers taken from a suit, even in his workshop, he seemed no different from usual.

'Houghton Conquest,' Father Ashley was saying, one bony finger extended towards the old-fashioned map of Bedfordshire hanging above the sofa. 'It was Houghton Conquest.' He was a gently spoken man, much admired in the village for being both 'a gentleman' and 'a good listener'. Prerequisites, it was agreed, for the priesthood. The only ungentle thing about him being a shock of spiky grey hair, which could have done with some of Mosa's smoothing.

'Your drink, Father,' said Douglas, handing the priest a tinkling glass. 'Say if you want more ice.'

'Thank you,' said Father Ashley, turning from the map. He took a sip, nodded approvingly, then continued, 'It was the Church of All Saints, one of the largest in the county, and he was curate there for maybe a year before he came to me.' Here he noticed Paul and added, 'Hello, young man! How's school? Keeping up all right? Have you found Simon?'

Three

'He's on the front stoep, dear,' said Peggy. 'Bored stiff, poor creature, by us grown-ups. A cooldrink? Then you can join him.'

'Coming up!' said Douglas. 'But this time I'll go easy on the gin.'

'Darling, honestly!' Peggy gave a reproving laugh. 'What will Father Ashley think!'

But Father Ashley was thinking only of a church in Bedfordshire. 'Anyway, as I was saying, there are some patches of wall painting that are fifteenth-century or thereabouts, which he showed me once, and some very old glass in some of the windows and a rather fine family tomb – Purbeck marble, if I'm remembering right – with some brasses of the Conquest family.'

'That okay?' asked Douglas, passing Paul his cooldrink. 'I've gone so easy on the gin you won't even taste it. But there's always more ice.'

'I'll ring when lunch is ready,' said Peggy crisply. 'Not long now. Promise.'

'That's what I miss,' said Father Ashley, still following his own train of thought. 'The sense of history. People here think our church is old just because it dates from 1924. Whereas we – we have a different sense of these things. Don't we, Peggy? Douglas? Delicious gin, by the way.'

Douglas had filled Paul's glass to the brim and so, since he didn't want to spill anything on the parquet, once out of the lounge he paused to take a sip and thus heard, 'But, going back to Simon, what will you do?' The voice was Peggy's. '*Such* a worry. If only Evelyn were still alive.'

Paul was tempted to linger – this sounded intriguing – except he knew that, if he did, he risked either Mosa appearing from the kitchen to tell Peggy she was ready to serve, or Peggy materialising in search of Mosa. So instead, he pushed on.

The front stoep was triangular in shape and, unlike the long one at the side of the house, fairly small, taking Mosa only minutes to polish in the mornings. A low brick wall surrounded it, on which was perched a scowling Simon.

Like his father, Simon was lean and had noteworthy hair – in his case, an elaborate quiff, which to Paul was a wonder: that a man's hair could be swept up like that! And stay there! But here any similarity ended, for, where Father Ashley was gentle in manner, Simon was so intense that when he fixed you with his brooding gaze it felt as though his eyes were pinning you to the spot.

'So what's the old man saying now?' he demanded as Paul appeared. 'Has he told them about Jean's letter? God! I can just imagine.'

'Letter? What letter?' Setting his cooldrink down beside him, Paul joined Simon on the wall. 'Who's Jean?'

'You mean he's holding back for once? Even with your sainted mother? Shit, dare I believe you?'

Taking care not to show surprise at the swear word – after all, he didn't want to discourage Simon from treating him as an equal – Paul said cautiously, 'He was talking about some boring old church, actually. Though afterwards I did hear Mum say ... '

'What?'

Three

'Something about you being a worry. And *if only your own mum was still around* ... But I was in the passage by then and —'

'So he has bloody told them! The bastard! A girl writes a private letter – private, hey! Strictly private – to her boyfriend, where she talks about things they've done together. Private things, okay? Well, that's until some self-righteous old fart comes along, thinking he has the right to open the letter just because the boyfriend has recently joined NUSAS and the dean has written to all parents to say he doesn't approve of NUSAS and its campaigns. Talk about a police state!'

From this, Paul understood (but only just) that someone (Father Ashley, it had to be Father Ashley) had opened a letter of Simon's, written by his girlfriend, Jean. Though quite what the 'private things' were, he couldn't imagine. Nor why Simon had chosen to talk about himself in the third person. And 'NUSAS'? This really stumped him.

Asking, he was told brusquely, 'The National Union of South African Students, duh! God! Don't they teach you anything at that stuck-up school of yours?' Followed by, 'The most natural thing in the world, some would say sacred, but they treat it as dirty. They're the ones who need watching, not me.'

If I'd been older, I'd have immediately got what he was referring to. The twelve-year-old Paul, however, had no idea; and anyway, by now he was tiring of Simon's company and was not displeased when, moments later, they heard the tinkle of the bell that stood, in the shape of a miniature brass shepherdess, on the dining room sideboard. Lunch was served.

'Don't forget your cooldrink,' said Simon as they both stood up.

The dining room was located between the lounge and the kitchen; gloomily too, having just the one, rather small window, unlike the lounge and kitchen, which had two apiece. Nor was there much here to soften the severe lines of the oak table with its six straight-backed chairs and matching sideboard, unless you counted the black and white prints on the walls, which in any case were fairly grotesque, the work of someone called Hogarth. Though most telling of all, to Paul's mind, was that in this room the otherwise cheery Mosa always seemed so subdued, forever hovering in attendance by the sideboard, waiting for Douglas, once he'd carved, to hand her the plate so that she, in turn, could set it before its intended recipient.

'Ah, Simon!' said Douglas, looking up from his carving. 'You'll have a drumstick, I'm sure. *And* some breast? I was never a student myself, but I do remember my appetite as a young man. Appetites, indeed.'

'Douglas! Really!'

'Actually, Mr Harvey,' said Simon, taking the place opposite his father, 'last term I became a vegetarian.'

Peggy let out an anguished cry. 'Simon!' she wailed, and to Father Ashley, 'You might have warned us! I would have made macaroni cheese or something.'

Father Ashley just shrugged. 'Don't distress yourself, Peggy, my dear,' he said. 'Tomorrow it'll be another fad.'

Three

'I'm fine with only vegetables,' confirmed Simon. 'Honestly, Mrs Harvey. I'm used to it.'

'Now would you like me to say grace?' continued the priest coolly. 'Once Douglas is done.'

'Oh, would you, Father?' said Peggy, adding for Paul's benefit, 'That's right, dear. You're next to me. And do make yourself useful.' She nodded towards the gravy boat.

Douglas, meanwhile, had finished carving and was telling Mosa, 'Madam will ring for pudding.'

As the door closed on the uniformed back of the departing server, Father Ashley began his benediction, intoning it in a domestic version of the voice he used in the pulpit; softer, but no less sonorous. His preacher's voice, Douglas called it, though never in Peggy's hearing.

'Amen!'

When guests weren't present, in between whatever they might have to say to each other, Peggy and Douglas would always ask Paul about his week and what was happening at school; or, if it was the holidays, they'd talk about how he should amuse himself, what outings were in store. But when guests were around Paul might as well have been absent. Except that he wasn't, of course; he was absorbing, if not always understanding, every word.

The talk began with Marilyn Monroe. An actress, seemingly, who'd just died. Rather young and in suspicious circumstances. There was going to be a commemorative season of her films at the drive-in. Douglas hoped they might go. He liked how she'd sung happy birthday to President Kennedy. They'd seen it in a newsreel.

This prompted Simon to ask whether anyone realised that other, more important things were happening in America just now. Paul guessed at once where this might be leading: James Meredith no doubt and the riots in Mississippi. In relation to which, Father Ashley spoke at some length, and in his preacher's voice again, about human decency, or the lack of it, and other people's civil rights.

Simon, however, soon brought the conversation round to South Africa. 'If we're going to talk about civil rights ... ' He referred to something called the Sabotage Act, which had apparently been passed a few months previously. The act carried, he said, a minimum sentence of five years. Five years! A maximum one of death. Death! Not to mention its provisions for banning people and placing them under a sinister new form of arrest: house arrest. All because they might say things the government didn't want said. Believe things the government didn't want people to believe. Like, for instance, civil rights for all.

'Simon, really!' said Father Ashley. 'Next you'll be attacking the Suppression of Communism Act!'

'Yes, and I really hope, dear,' proffered Peggy, 'you don't mean us to stop fighting communism? That would be very short-sighted.'

Here Douglas drew their attention to someone by the name of Nelson Mandela, who'd been on the run, by the sound of it, but had recently been arrested on a road in Natal and was about to be brought to trial for leaving the country illegally, without a passport, and for inciting a strike.

'We have to remember,' he said, 'that this ANC of his supports acts of sabotage. Like that bomb in the centre of Johannesburg earlier this year which that other man – I forget the name – has just been sentenced for.'

'Turok,' said Simon. 'Benjamin Turok.'

'You can't expect the government to stand idly by. We don't want anarchy.'

'Yes, but Mr Harvey, that strike he organised – and he had to go into hiding to do even that – it was only to protest at the new republic and our racial laws. And if you halfway agree, Dad, about civil rights in America, then surely—'

'This country, Simon, is different,' snapped Father Ashley. 'South Africa has its own unique set of problems and I, for one, don't feel I have the right – I wasn't born here, remember – to tell those who were how to run their own country. That's for them to decide.'

'Hear, hear!' said Peggy.

'So maybe South Africa *is* a special case,' conceded Simon. 'But you still enjoy its privileges. And anyway, I *was* born here, and if you listen to what NUSAS has to say ... '

'NUSAS!' exclaimed Father Ashley. 'You really mean to introduce NUSAS into the conversation after everything we've endured this week? Sometimes I despair of you, Simon, really I do.'

Now it was Peggy's turn to interrupt. 'Paul, dear, don't forget to put your knife and fork together. That's right. Then be a poppet and pass the bell.'

While Father Ashley added sorrowfully, 'This must be so boring for you, I do apologise.'

'Well, actually, Father,' countered Paul, pushing back his chair, 'we learned about James Meredith in school this week.'

'Really?' queried Peggy. 'How?'

'With Mr Spier. In General Knowledge.'

'Spier?' said Simon, perking up. 'Andrew Spier? Used to be at Wits?'

'Funny!' said Douglas. 'We were talking at cricket yesterday and he said he knew you. Small world!'

Paul handed Peggy the brass shepherdess, which she instantly started ringing for Mosa to clear away their plates and bring in the pudding.

'I hope you've left enough room,' she said, 'all of you.'

'And *I* hope, Simon,' said Douglas, 'that after lunch I can show you the race track I've built for Paul. Maybe you'll be more impressed by it than he seems to be. Or am I doing you a disservice, old fruit?'

The door was pushed open and through it bustled Mosa with her tray, on which stood a Queen of Puddings, its meringue topping a dramatic mountainscape of snowy white tinged, on some of its slopes, to a delectable brown.

'Gosh, but you spoil us, Peggy,' sighed Father Ashley. 'Really you do.'

After lunch, while Douglas steered Simon towards the garage and Peggy dragged Father Ashley into the garden to discuss what she might try growing there, Paul went as usual to his room to rest. In earlier times, Peggy had insisted that for this part of the day he strip down to his underpants and actually get into bed, under the covers, with the curtains drawn. Nowadays, however, he was considered old enough to manage his own movements and would generally spend the time updating his precious diary. This he kept safely at the back of his cupboard, alongside his old teddy and the only comics Peggy would allow. *Classics Illustrated*, they were called. *Featuring Stories by the World's Greatest Authors*. He owned perhaps half a dozen, the cover of each one an arresting image of the story within, his favourite by far being *A Tale of Two Cities*, which showed a frock-coated Sydney Carton, hands tied behind his back, staring gallantly heavenwards while behind him could be glimpsed the waiting guillotine and an implacable executioner, aproned and at the ready.

'It is a far, far better thing that I do,' Carton had said on his way to death, 'than I have ever done; it is a far, far better rest that I go to than I have ever known.'

Seeing himself, secretly at least, as a victim of history too, Paul reacted fervently to these words. Always had. By identifying with Carton, even though he couldn't pretend to be as brave, he could nonetheless permit himself a certain glamour. A certain stoicism. Much needed on occasion.

Freeing his diary, he took it to his desk, unlocked it, and began to leaf through its creamy pages, reading as he went, until he came at last to the required date.

But what to write there? How to encapsulate all that had happened during the previous week? None of his earlier entries about du Toit had involved such complexity.

Should he mistrust his new 'friend'? Or regard past behaviour as … well, as a sort of reflex, he supposed, a muscular spasm beyond du Toit's control. Maybe du Toit did things like stealing Paul's diary because he couldn't help himself. Was horrible without meaning to be. Maybe, when all was said and done, as du Toit's new friend … Amazing! *And* they'd all been invited to visit by Mr du Toit – Paul didn't need to continue fearing him.

Eyes straying to the Kipling poem that hung, framed, on the wall above his desk, he wondered how he could ever hope to fit all of this into the seven small rectangles the diary allowed, while still leaving room for such staples as his marks and the tuck he'd taken into school? But if he didn't start soon he would never finish – and so, unscrewing his pen, he began to set down his version of the week's strange encounters. His and no one else's.

It took him quite some time, but eventually he was done and it was with a degree of satisfaction that he turned the page to the week starting Monday, October 8th, which he marked with the ribbon attached to the diary for that purpose. Then he closed and carefully locked his most treasured possession before finally returning it to the guardianship of Teddy, the company of the doomed yet dashing Sydney Carton.

Four

'A FINE, I SEE,' said Mrs MacWilliam as Paul approached her desk, overdue book held before him. 'Though tell you what: if you can put it back for me yourself, *and* those over there on the trolley, I might just let you off. Deal?'

Homely by nature, and kindly-looking, she had a mess of greying hair that was always escaping its bun, while her features, which lacked sharpness anyway, tended to be smudged rather than defined by her make-up. Her smile was imprecise too; and her glasses, when not on her nose, were invariably to be found aslant the shelf of her ample bosom, held there by a fraying cord looped negligently about her neck. Yet, despite appearances, Mrs MacWilliam was a stickler for order when it came to her library. Each of the books she'd indicated to Paul to put away was neatly covered in sturdy plastic and bore a label in the centre of its spine, coloured and numbered according to subject matter. And as Paul began to return these books to the shelves which stretched from floor to ceiling across all four of the library's walls – he'd accepted Mrs MacWilliam's offer with alacrity, since his parents kept him on a pretty tight leash, money-wise – he thought again how safe the library always made him feel; how cocooned. Partly because it was so well-ordered; but also because its shelves muffled all trace of outside noise, even from the nearby kitchen. Only some of the smells got through, making its embrace – its musty, dusty, dimly lit embrace – infinitely soothing.

'You are an obliging boy!' said Mrs MacWilliam before he'd quite finished. 'I wonder … Mrs Stanford and I have been thinking about getting ourselves a library monitor. It wouldn't involve much. Just an extra pair of hands, really. Once or twice a week. Well?'

Paul had, he realised, put away upwards of fifteen books in half that many minutes. Just one remained, a novel (the colour of the label told him that) about flies, of all things. Hardly arduous, then, being a library monitor, and he did like it here. So why not? But, before he could say as much, he became aware of another presence in the room. The obsequious Slug, no less. Who must have slipped in quietly, while Mrs MacWilliam had been talking.

'Well, dear?' said Mrs MacWilliam.

'What do *you* want?' demanded Paul of the new arrival.

'We're waiting,' said Slug. 'Didn't he tell you?'

'Now, now, boys!' came the inevitable if gentle reprimand. 'This *is* the library.'

Four

'Come on!' said Slug impatiently, beseeching Paul with magnified eyes. 'He'll get even crosser if we don't go quick.'

'If you're not here to borrow a book, young man, then I suggest—'

'Okay,' hissed Paul. 'Keep your hair on.' And to Mrs MacWilliam, 'Can I come back later to talk about it?'

'Of course you can, dear.' Mrs MacWilliam smiled. 'Though don't leave it too long, all right?'

'*Dear*!' remarked Slug with a sly grin as, moments later, they dashed across the playground. 'She called you *dear*!'

'So what?' retorted Paul. 'Just because no one talks nicely to you!'

The tuck shop, he noted gratefully, had closed its doors for the day and there were few observers about. Ditto for the playing fields, where – since games were over – the only potential watcher was a distant Pheko, bent low over his roller as he inched it across the pitch.

Ever since the weekend, when his parents' questions had, in conjunction with the unexpected introduction of Mr du Toit into the equation, caused Paul to scrutinise his feelings more than he might have otherwise, his initial delight at being asked to join du Toit's club had been compromised by a growing unease. Could you, he'd been forced to speculate, be mistaken in your own desires? Nor was his unease lessened by the summons from Slug. So okay, the moment of initiation – long hankered after – had presumably arrived. But why Slug, whom no one in their right mind wanted ever, under any circumstances, to be seen with?

'There's space,' du Toit had said, 'is all.'

Involving whom, though? Not Slug, it would seem, because if Slug had been sent to summon Paul he must currently be du Toit's right-hand man. Wasn't that how it worked?

So had Lombard been displaced in that case? And, if so, how? Why? When?

'We'd better go round,' panted the object of Paul's reflections, pointing at the distant Pheko. 'Or he'll report us.'

The hut where du Toit held court was on the far side of the fields, in a long, narrow ditch that marked the boundary between the school grounds and the outside world. Here, in an irregular row, were half a dozen such huts, all built from scrap wood, sheets of corrugated iron, branches and whatever else the builders had been able to lay their hands on. Most were pretty basic and cramped – Paul had been inside one once. But some were larger and boasted superior features like a strip of old carpet, rudimentary windows, a hinged door. Du Toit's was one of these and, as Paul and Slug slithered down the side of the ditch towards it, Paul noticed that against the door – an actual door with an actual doorknob wonkily attached to it – was propped a clipboard with a piece of paper on it and a chewed pencil dangling from one of its corners.

Still panting, Slug took up the clipboard and demanded, 'Name?'

Paul looked at Slug in some amazement.

'I need you to say it,' wheezed Slug, tapping the clipboard. 'It's the rules.'

Ah! thought Paul. *The rules.*

'Okay,' he said grudgingly. 'Paul Harvey.'

'Is that your only name?'

'Of course not.'

'The rules say "in full". I'll show you if you like.'

'Okay,' said Paul again, although he didn't like this one bit. 'Paul Thomas Barnabas Harvey.' The Barnabas was for his grandmother's father, or so he'd once been told; he never used it himself, not even when first inscribing his diary. It was just too weird and might all too easily lead, he'd always feared, to teasing.

So why had he proffered it, then? Why hadn't he stopped at Thomas? No one would have been any the wiser.

Meanwhile, Slug was knocking on the door – four distinct times – saying between each knock: (knock) 'I…' (knock) '…ask…' (knock) '…permission.' (knock).

The knocks had no immediate effect, however, other than causing the doorknob to wobble, and a few anxious moments passed before, finally, they heard an answering murmur from within.

'Enter,' said Slug, taking careful hold of the doorknob. 'And duck, hey, or you'll catch the support and the hut will collapse. It has happened.'

Paul did as instructed, with Slug following close behind, to be met by a pervasive smell of earthy decay and damp. Then he saw, taking gradual shape in the gloom – for du Toit's hut didn't have a window, just the door, which Slug had closed behind them – a clutch of shadowy forms: Horton, Strover, Labuschagne and Kintock. So! It *was* Lombard who'd been chucked out (clever, popular Lombard), putting Slug (wobbly, ridiculous, pitiful, bespectacled Slug) in the ascendant.

Whatever next!

The club members were all crouched at the feet of their captain, who himself was not on his haunches but sat on an upturned wooden crate. On his head was a plastic Roman helmet, part of some dressing-up set by the look of it, while behind him, against the wall of rusty corrugated iron, hung a shabby strip of carpet on which had been painted, in white, a series of interlocking rings, rather like the Olympic symbol, except here there were six rings, not five. One for each member of the club, presumably.

'Greet the new boy!' commanded du Toit, raising an imperious hand.

'Welcome, Harvey!' chanted the others. 'Paul Thomas Barnabas Harvey: welcome.'

So this was why Slug had coerced him into revealing all of his names!

Du Toit then ordered his right-hand man to read the rules.

Slug had regained his breath by now and so, clipboard to hand, was able to recite them in a measured monotone, much like someone standing on the dais in Stanford's maths class, reciting theorems.

One: The captain must be obeyed at all times.
Two: The captain must be referred to only by
         rank, never by name.

Three: Whenever he wishes, the captain may set
club members tasks to perform so that the
member can retain or improve his ranking
within the club.

Four: Club members must not talk to non-club
members about the club's activities.

Five: Meetings are to be held at least once a week
and in the club house.

Six: Members may only speak at meetings when
invited to do so by the captain.

There was more, but by now Paul had rather stopped
listening. Rule number one had made the general point and
anyway, what about his task, he was thinking, assuming
he'd be set one? That trumped rules, which he reckoned he
could swot up any time, like you did homework.

Slug finished his recital – as with the Biblical
commandments, there were ten in all – and the captain
now asked for something called the minutes: a round-up
of recent activities, this turned out to be, some of which
Slug talked about from notes attached to his clipboard,
others of which various club members reported on.
Labuschagne and Kintock, for instance, told of a joint
task they'd been set – they did everything together, these
two: giggled as one in class, had adjoining beds in the
dormitory, hooks likewise for their towels in the shower
room. And last week they'd also been the ones to apple-
pie the juniors' beds.

'During morning break,' explained Labuschagne.
'That's when we did it.'

'Matron's never around then – we had spans of time,' added Kintock eagerly. 'So we did the whole dormitory, not just Biccard's, like you said.'

Clearly he was expecting du Toit to be impressed by this show of zeal. Instead of which, a chilling silence descended, broken at length by the captain leaning forward and saying, 'If I want you to show initiative, Kintock, I'll tell you in advance. Okay?'

Paul wondered whether Kintock might protest, the put-down had been that severe; but in the gloom it was impossible to read anyone's expression with accuracy: eyes were simply pools of further darkness against areas of ghost-like glimmer. And besides, du Toit didn't give him time.

'Right, Murray,' he was saying, using Slug's surname. 'Harvey comes in over Labuschagne and Kintock. Got that?'

Consulting his clipboard, Slug confirmed: 'One: Murray. Two: Strover. Three: Horton. Four: Harvey. Five: Labuschagne. Six: Kintock.'

'Number four,' said du Toit, turning to Paul with a satisfied nod. 'And if you do your first task okay, you'll go even further. The only limit is yourself. Isn't that right, everyone?'

'Yes, captain!' chorused the others.

'What are we?'

'Your club!'

'What do we do?'

'Work together!'

'Who do we fear?'

'No one!'

'And who do we follow?'

'You, captain!'

As imperiously as before, du Toit held up his hand once more.

'Club dismissed,' he said. 'All except Harvey.'

'But you haven't told him his task!' objected Slug.

'What?'

'His task. You haven't—'

'Are you questioning me, Murray?'

'No, captain, of course not. But usually you—'

'So today things are different. That's all. Okay?'

There was an awkward pause, at the tail-end of which Slug said meekly, 'Yes, captain. Sorry, captain. It won't happen again. Promise.'

Still crouching – within the confines of the hut, it was impossible to do otherwise – he then crept towards the door and pushed it open. The others all exited, dipping their heads in the direction of their captain as they went, while the chastened Slug ticked off their names on his list before finally exiting himself.

The door was pushed shut and Paul was alone in the gloom with his nemesis. A less than comfortable experience, he discovered. Desired maybe, but not exactly delightful.

Oh, he could just imagine what his parents might say!

'Captain?' His voice sounded strange, even to his own ears.

In a low tone, du Toit said, 'I sent the others away because the task I have for you is secret. No one must know. Next time we're in Spier's study, if you see anything unusual, I want you to *gap* it. Okay? Then bring it to me. Got that?'

Or words to this effect because it's more Paul's utter surprise at being tasked with stealing something from Spier that lingers in the memory. He knew of course that du Toit didn't care for Spier, that Spier was hard on du Toit. But to want something stolen from Spier's study? What would that achieve?

It was all most odd – Lombard having been chucked out, Slug now being du Toit's right-hand man, the nature of his task – all without precedent and liable, you might have thought, to give him pause as he emerged afterwards into the dying light of day. Except it didn't. Rather, the sharp unease he'd been feeling earlier began gradually to evaporate as he made his slow way back to the main building and was gone completely – like magic, *poof!* – by the time he'd reached the playground. He could even have sworn that the boys gathering there to go into supper were regarding him with new respect.

And why not? After all, he had now been fully inducted into his new status. Hadn't he?

Remembering again how glorious it felt, this sensation of walking tall for a change, I arrive, unambushed, at the outskirts of the town I've been aiming for. In the dark, I can just about make out a sign saying welcome; also, an almost unpronounceable and most unusual-sounding name. Unremembered too; not even faintly familiar. When last I'd looked in any detail at an atlas of the country – with MacWilliam in geography, most probably – towns like this had generally been Afrikaans by designation, never African.

If that's the correct distinction to make. Because aren't both choices, in their way, African? I should really say Sotho; or Tswana; or Zulu; or whatever language it is that's been used to rename the town.

Mokimolle.

It sounds like a dip.

What hasn't altered, though, is the 'feel' of the place. Its unmistakable type, evident even in the dark. The single main street with its tatty shops and commercial buildings, all grouped within a few blocks of each other. And, beyond this, a couple more blocks, but no more than a couple, of uniform bungalows, also tatty-looking, one of which must house my B&B. Then further veld, vastly more veld, and an abiding sense therefore that the town's existence is vestigial.

'So you're from Sussex!' says Giles, the B&B's owner, as he signs me in. 'I've been to Sussex. Brighton. I really liked Brighton. Though you have to laugh, hey, when they call it a beach. Those pebbles. I mean!'

I learn too that Giles lives with Lawrence, whom I will meet later – right now he's cooking – and that they started their B&B after retiring early from stressful jobs in Gauteng.

'Five years this October,' explains Giles, 'and we haven't looked back. I used to like Jozie – sorry, I mean Johannesburg. That's what we call it here. Best city in the world, I used to say, but the country's changed, hey. It's really changed.' With plump hands, he smooths his billowy shirt, worn loose, I guess, in the hope of disguising his bulk, although if anything it encourages the eye towards it. 'But you don't want me *gaaning aan* about Jozie when what you must be craving is a hot shower, a stiff drink and, after, a delicious dinner. You'll see: Lawrence is an ace chef. Come, let me show you your room.'

The B&B is in just the sort of bungalow I'd been expecting. Its interior, however, comes as quite a shock, for in terms of décor Giles and Lawrence are of my mother's persuasion. They too favour chintz, Persian rugs, a plethora of ornaments, in their case with a camp twist – they've accessorised their chintz with any number of fussy, beribboned cushions, their curtains are extravagantly swagged and ruched, their ornaments, copper and brass mainly, glister; and where Peggy had favoured neutral paint tones for the walls they've plumped for racing green, some burgundy and a good deal of pink. Even in the room to which I'm now shown, swathes of a flowery fabric are looped about the bed; the paintings are of idealised English landscapes, meadows dotted with cows, sun-dappled streams, that sort of thing; while in the en-suite bathroom there are period-looking tiles and taps, not to mention a bar or two of curlicued soap.

'I hope you'll be comfortable,' says the beaming owner. 'Because that's our aim. To make our guests feel completely, but *completely* at home.'

Then out he sidles as I collapse with a groan on to the bed, closing my eyes against the faux European clutter hemming me in. What an irony, to have chosen this particular B&B! In the end, I have indeed been ambushed. Not by any section of the rainbow nation, though. It's the ever-present past that's crept up on me again.

No escaping, either, how quickly the next General Knowledge session came round, giving Paul little time in which to enjoy walking tall before he had somehow to confront and perform his task.

'Nelson Mandela,' Spier was saying. 'Who's heard of Nelson Mandela?'

'I have, sir,' said Paul, in happy possession for once of an answer. 'Wasn't he arrested recently in Natal?'

Spier was equally delighted.

'Well, well!' he said. 'Does this mean you've actually been reading the papers for a change? You and who else? Or is it just that your parents discuss things at home? How many of you discuss politics at home? Hands up!'

No one obliged, of course – they never did respond to challenges of this nature – causing Spier, who was lounging against his untidy desk as usual, to look searchingly at each of them in turn.

'Because I've been thinking,' he continued, brown eyes pensive, 'that the moment has maybe come for us to look more closely at our own fair land. Last May we were made a republic. Why, exactly? What were the steps we took in cutting loose like this from the Commonwealth, setting ourselves up as a separate country? Well?'

But again no one ventured a word, so after a prolonged and increasingly awkward silence he began to provide the details himself. With a sigh, he took them back to 1948, when the nationalist government had first come to power. He highlighted the introduction of apartheid, group areas, pass laws and something called suffrage. He also talked about things that had been touched on for Paul at Sunday lunch, like the Suppression of Communism Act; or, from earlier, the State of Emergency the government had declared following the massacre at Sharpeville.

The last of these events, not only Paul but the others too could all remember from the vivid photos that had accompanied the many newspaper articles on the subject; photos of policemen standing guard outside their police station while the protestors (black, naturally) fled the shots that had just been fired. Plus, in Paul's case, there had been the fallout at home. The letters – even, at one point, a tearful phone call – from his grandmother. His mother's angry, anguished response. His father saying, as Father Ashley had, that people who weren't born in South Africa, or didn't live here, couldn't know the whole story; shouldn't pass judgement.

Meanwhile, Spier wanted to know what the following letters stood for – PAC? ANC? – arriving by this route at the aforementioned Mandela, whose trial was about to be held, he told them, in the Old Synagogue. 'In other words, on our very doorstep.'

Four

'But, sir,' interrupted Horton, 'isn't a synagogue where Jewish people go to worship?'

'*Ja*, it's that really weird-looking building,' said Bentley major, 'in Paul Kruger Street. We drive past it going home.'

'The design,' said Spier, 'is Byzantine.'

'So why there, sir,' asked Horton, 'if it's not really a court?'

'Ah, but it is,' crowed Spier. 'That's the funny thing. The government acquired it years ago and have recently been using it, quite cleverly in my opinion, as somewhere to try cases that involve national security. It's far enough away from Jo'burg, see, to make it difficult for supporters to come all this way and sit in the gallery. The government isn't stupid.'

Did he really say all that? Possibly not – Paul's mind was more on his looming task – although during this session he certainly made coded mention of du Toit's note from the week before.

'Last time,' was how he did it, going to stand behind du Toit's Brylcreemed head, 'one of you indicated that he'd like to know more about what some call *die rooi gevaar*. A subject we have, of course, considered before. Countries like North Vietnam and Cuba. Why the West gets so exercised. Well, by following this trial, which I promise we will, and asking ourselves – without prejudice, mind – why our government behaves as it does, we might just start to see a pattern here.'

Then Lombard, glasses glinting, performed his usual trick.

'Supper, sir,' he cried, 'in ten minutes. And it's Mr Stanford, sir, on duty tonight.'

Paul's eyes, in the interim, were locked on Spier's desk. *Next time we're in Spier's study, if you see anything unusual...*

What, though? And where? How would he ever manage, in the stampede for the door, to lift anything of any description from the chaos on Spier's desk?

Chairs were being pushed back. Spier was moving towards the door. Everyone was standing up. Except, that was, for du Toit, who said, from where he was sitting, 'Sir, there's a book, sir, I was wondering if I could borrow. There by the door. Can I, sir? Please?'

Cover! He was trying to provide cover. Something Paul hadn't imagined would be on offer. But how brilliant that it was! He must make the most of it. So, while du Toit looked with Spier for some quite spurious book and the others all stepped around them, Paul began scanning the confusion on Spier's desk for what it might yield. Exercise books and old newspapers mainly; countless pens and pencils and rubber bands and... but what was that, peeking out from under some papers? A comb? Some sort of comb? It had teeth like a comb, although they were, it had to be said, unusually large. Also, the object was of wood and square-shaped, where combs tended to be oblong and of plastic. So highly unusual, then, exactly as stipulated, and in less time than it took for du Toit to tell Spier it was okay if they couldn't find the book, perhaps by next session he'd have remembered better what it looked like, Paul had slipped the object into his pocket.

'I don't want you thinking that what you do goes unnoticed,' said Spier seconds later, as he stepped away from the desk to head for the door. 'Hear me, Harvey?'

Paul's stomach lurched. Did Spier maybe have what his mother boasted of having: eyes in the back of his head? But no, apparently and luckily not, since what he then said was, 'You made a real contribution today. Thank you.'

Words which, at any other time, Paul would have savoured, committed to his diary even, but which in the present circumstances he was simply too flustered to register fully. All he managed, as he squirmed past, was a mumbled, 'Yes, sir, I do try, sir, I hope you know that.'

Stanford's daughters had, since the previous week, cleared away their playthings, leaving nothing on the lawn except an expectant du Toit.

'You must never tell,' he warned as Paul came up to him, 'that I tried to help, okay? You do things on your own. Got that?'

Then, without waiting for Paul to fall in alongside him – or say even whether he had in the end been able to find anything of note on Spier's desk – he darted away, and by the time Paul himself emerged from the masters' compound was halfway round the open expanse of the fields already, a diminishing arrangement of collapsed grey socks, trim grey shorts, white shirt and a flash of purple tie; while from the centre of the nearest field was approaching a contrasting arrangement of baggy and, in this instance, khaki shorts, no socks (bare feet, in fact) and a khaki shirt that gaped not only at the neck, but wherever it happened to be torn. Pheko, the school groundsman, who would also be bringing with him the pungent smell of that other compound, the one where the servants lived: a smell of Lifebuoy, the soap provided by the school for all its inmates, combined, in Pheko's case, with tobacco, wood-smoke and a young man's sweat. Though, as the groundsman was still at some distance, Paul didn't actually have to experience anything other than the sight of him before he, too, began running towards the main building.

In line for supper, he had time at last to catch his breath, order his thoughts and remind himself that these days – remember, remember! – he was walking tall. A member – number four, no less – of the school's most select grouping. *Mustn't panic. Hold your head high. Sydney Carton style.*

Then up sidled Slug and, although Paul did wonder why it should be necessary to do this now, rather than at the next club meeting, he nevertheless found himself – quite proudly, too – obliging Slug in his request by passing him, in all its strangeness, the object he'd lifted from Spier's desk. Having first made sure, of course, that Stanford wasn't looking.

'People don't always do so well,' murmured Slug with a surprised smile as he pocketed Paul's offering. 'You'll go far, man.'

Both my hosts are in evidence as I enter the dining room, which I do through double doors at one end of it, doors which must have been closed on my arrival at the B&B, since I don't remember glimpsing the room earlier. Not that it looks any different from the rest of the house. The curtains are every bit as swagged and ruched; again there are Persian carpets on the floor, more English scenes of a pastoral nature on the pink walls. Only the immaculately set tables, four in all, each unoccupied, distinguish the room.

'Ah!' cries Giles, swooping forward like a bulky ballerina; past her sell-by date maybe, but still fleet of foot. 'There you are! We were wondering.'

He has a different shirt on, although, as with the décor, it doesn't exactly ring the changes. Also flowered, also flowing, on a smaller person it could have doubled as a dress.

'Take this table here, why not?' he continues, pulling out a chair. 'Plenty choice tonight. No other guests. Then Lawrence'll fix you a drink. What'll you have? There's everything – hey, Lawrence!'

Lawrence is not as tall as Giles, or as voluminous. He's bird-like rather and has a sharp, enquiring face. He extends a quick hand. 'Welcome to Mokimolle,' he says. 'First time? You must take a walk in the morning, see it by daylight. From the *koppie* – it's not far – you get really *lekker* views.'

'But first a drink!' interrupts Giles. 'Let the poor *ou* order himself a drink, *skattie*, his tongue must be hanging out, while I tell him what's on the menu.'

I order some wine and the *bobotie*. Then, left alone to continue my wry assessment of the room while they attend to my wants, it occurs to me that, as I'm dining alone, I'll probably be required, when the food comes, to give an account of myself. And so it transpires: once Giles has overseen a uniformed waiter in the setting down on my table of what I've ordered, and Lawrence has produced and opened a bottle of wine, even though the pair of them could now withdraw, they don't.

'You must forgive me!' sighs Giles, closing the door to the kitchen on the departing waiter's back. 'But unless you watch their every move...'

'How's the wine?' Lawrence cuts in, sensing, from my look, that the subject could do with changing. 'One thing at least that this country does get right, hey!'

Again I nod, then add for his further benefit that the *bobotie* is delicious.

'Something else,' he says with a pleased smile, 'special to us. It's from Malaysia. Slaves introduced it. Way back when.'

'*Ag, nee!*' says Giles, rolling his eyes. 'Don't get him started on *blerrie* history, else we'll be here all night.'

'Oh dear, are we being insensitive?' says Lawrence, a look of sudden concern replacing his smile. 'Would you rather be alone? Should we go?'

To which I feel I can only reply, 'No, no, of course not. Company's always welcome.'

'Are you sure?'

Another, hopefully convincing nod.

Whereupon Giles suggests to Lawrence that he fetch their own bottle of wine and the two of them are very soon settled at the table alongside mine.

Four

For a while, the talk remains general. The weather, the state of the roads out of Jozie, the sad fact that people don't dare use the railways any more.

'Well, *we* wouldn't, *you* wouldn't,' says Giles. 'It's just not safe and they used to be so good. *Ag*, this country!'

In this way we arrive at the moment of truth. They're keen to know when I got here. Have I just flown in? Where am I headed? Will I be with them only the one night, or am I staying in the area longer? People, do, they say. It has attractions.

They're going on my accent, of course. Plus how pale I am.

And I don't disabuse them. I pretend this is indeed my first visit. I'm English, I say. A veritable pom. I play up fully to being European – not in the old, South African sense of the word, but insofar as this is where I hail from.

Nor do I let slip that in other ways, too, we are not dissimilar.

Five

THAT EXEAT, Paul was of course due at du Toit's farm. Not that you would have guessed this from du Toit's behaviour at breakfast. He gave absolutely no sign that soon he would be playing host and, when the meal was over, simply vanished, leaving Paul to emerge alone from the gloom of the corridor into the dazzle of the day's sunlight.

Even so, and despite a feeling in his stomach of a kind more usually associated with returning to school *after* an exeat, Paul continued to walk tall. So what if his exeat invitation had come about strangely and the prospect of it did frighten him rather? It was a clear improvement on the term – the years – before.

And another thing. Looking round for the du Toits' dusty white truck, he could also enjoy the fact that, for someone who'd always been rather ashamed of his own parents' car – a modest Cortina, too modest when set against other parental vehicles, frequently Mercedes or the like, bigger, flashier, more expensive – a truck, however dusty, was pretty thrilling. And there it was, too, parked just inside the gate.

Through its windscreen – though only dimly, because of the dust and having to squint against the dazzle – Paul could discern two heads. So! Somehow du Toit, in spite of his vanishing act, had got there before him. But on reaching the truck he found that the head alongside Mr du Toit's belonged to a girl – older, by the look of her, than her brother, because that was who she had to be: du Toit's sister. She had the same lustrous hair, scraped into a ponytail; the same faultless tan; the same aura of disdain.

He hadn't known there'd be a sister.

'Behind Laura, Paul, why don't you?' instructed Mr du Toit through the open window. 'Just yank the handle, it's a bit stiff, and shove any junk on the floor. Now where's that *blerrie* son of mine? He'll be late for his own funeral, that one, hey, Laura?'

If Laura agreed, she wasn't saying. She didn't even turn in Paul's direction. Only Mr du Toit's cat-like eyes followed him in the rear-view mirror as he clambered into the back of the truck and began clearing the seat of a spanner, an empty biscuit packet, an oily rag that would have disastrously stained his Sunday shorts.

Then the other door was jerked open.

'Hi, Pa. Hi, sis,' said du Toit, climbing in. 'What are we waiting for? The next Ice Age?'

And this was thrilling too: to be witnessing at close quarters how another family operated. Even down to such details as Laura being dressed in a school uniform herself: sky-blue, like her eyes, suggesting that she, too, was a boarder. You didn't often get to meet a 'saint', as pupils from nearby St Mary's were known.

Paul was being taken out of himself.

'Less of your cheek, young man, and more respect,' rebuked Mr du Toit as he threw the truck into gear. 'We have a guest, remember.'

At this, du Toit, who'd been clearing his own seat of the stuff that had accumulated there, glanced up and, to Paul's amazement, looked across at him and winked. Actually winked.

The du Toits' farm was to the north of Pretoria, ten or so miles beyond the freshest of the city's suburbs: uncharted territory for Paul. Usually when leaving town his parents would head south, either to Johannesburg to shop, or, if it was their annual holiday, towards the coast. Ramsgate or Margate or Southbroom. Oh, and once they'd driven due east, to the edge of a township called Mamelodi, to drop off Mosa because the buses weren't running.

That the road was therefore unfamiliar should have been thrilling too – except there wasn't, as it happened, much to absorb, apart from the occasional tree and stretches of parched earth as seen from a tarred road which soon became a dirt one. Hence the state of the truck. None of it looked fit for farming, about which Mr du Toit was lecturing them as they skimmed the bumpy road, leaving behind a widening plume of dust.

'Four greats,' he was saying. 'My great, great, great, great-grandfather. So five, hey, for Andre and Laura. He was with Paul Kruger on the trek and the farm was big back then – more than two hundred *morgen*. You know *mos* what a *morgen* is?'

Paul had to admit that he didn't.

'So okay, it's how much land a man can till with an ox in one morning. *Een more*. Or *morgen*, in Dutch or German. Somewhere between one and two acres, normally. Though over the years the farm has got smaller and smaller and we've been forced into other things. It's tough making a living from land like ours.'

They were turning through a gate, beyond which, on a slight rise, stood a commonplace bungalow.

'Right, you *ous*!' said Mr du Toit, bringing the truck to a halt beneath a blue gum. 'Let's see what Violet's got.'

With Mr du Toit at their head, the trio of youngsters trooped on to the long stoep fronting the bungalow. There they found that glasses of cooldrink had been poured for them, a plate of rusks set out. Laura helped herself, then ran quickly to the far end of the stoep to vanish through a door there. Meanwhile, Mr du Toit lit a cigarette from the packet he kept in his shirt pocket and inhaled deeply.

'While you're showing your guest around,' he said, smoke snaking from him, 'you can also do me a favour, hey, and look in on Tsebo.'

'*Ag nee*, Pa. Must I?'

There was a sudden, chilly pause.

'Really?' said Mr du Toit, voice rumblier than usual. 'Don't think that because you've got a guest you still can't get a *blerrie* good *klap*. Okay?'

No wink this time.

'Explain how I'm busy with some calls,' he continued, 'and there's people for lunch. He'll understand. I'll go tomorrow, tell him. Got that?'

Then he too walked off, leaving Paul and du Toit to their own devices.

Or should that be Andre, now they were no longer at school? Christian not surname. Was that what you did when you became friends outside? Paul wished he knew. But it hadn't happened before; and anyway, how could he say with confidence that they were proper friends? Early days. It was still early days. So, as he helped himself to a rusk and took a cautious sip of his cooldrink, he waited for his companion to speak first.

'Okay, Harvey,' began du Toit, answering Paul's unspoken question, 'Slug's shown me what you got.' Smiling, he too reached for refreshment. 'Of course you had help from me – which you really, really mustn't talk about, hey – I'm not supposed to help *anyone* with their task – but still: you did all right. And I bet there's more you can find. I haven't forgotten how you keep a diary. You're good at noticing things. So – just go on watching, *ja*? And write it down this time, what you find or see. I want a proper report, like in your diary, if there's anything. 'Cause isn't it quite weird, don't you think, that Spier should talk to us about this Mandela guy? Normally it's the outside world.' Ending with a sly, 'You also knew about this trial. How come?'

As with Spier in General Knowledge, I can't with certainty remember du Toit's exact words. But I do have the gist; the underlying thrust. I also recall how Paul felt, as he listened and sipped at his cooldrink and tried to bite into his rusk without exploding it into crumbs.

A memory too, quite clear, of explaining about Simon Tindall coming to lunch. How intently du Toit listened as I talked about the priest's problematic son.

'Your parents are also pretty weird,' he said when I'd done, 'having friends like that.'

Then, as if realising that what he'd said might be wounding – the first time he'd ever shown such consideration – he added quickly, 'But you didn't choose them, hey? All parents are weird in their different ways.'

Which allowed Paul to ask something he wouldn't have dared ask otherwise: where was du Toit's mother? His own would never have let so long elapse before emerging.

'*Ag*, she's not around,' said du Toit, face whitening beneath his tan. Clearly he didn't want to talk about her, and so Paul knew better than to pursue the subject. Du Toit wasn't someone you pushed.

A scraping sound distracted him. Mr du Toit, still wreathed in smoke, was scowling from a nearby window. 'Forgotten that *klap*?' he growled.

The sun was high in the sky, an intense white radiance that translated into an immediate prickle of sweat on the back of Paul's neck as he jumped from the stoep to follow du Toit, who was already halfway towards a cluster of outbuildings.

'Wait! Not so fast!'

Thus began their circuit of the farm, which certainly had shrunk in size from its original two hundred *morgen* or so; Mr du Toit hadn't been exaggerating. The outbuildings, for instance, numbered just four in total and were not much more, really, than large garages. A rusting car on bricks and a clutter of equally rusted agricultural machinery – ploughs and the like – occupied the first, while the second was locked, the third empty and the fourth home to just one pile of sacks.

'What's in those?'

'*Mielies*,' said du Toit, over his shoulder. 'But not ours, hey, we only store them for a neighbour.'

They'd started up a small *koppie* behind the outbuildings, which was where – as their pace slackened – Paul did finally manage to ask, since naturally this was intriguing him too, about Lombard. Why, he wanted to know, addressing du Toit's sweaty back, was Lombard no longer a friend? What had happened to cause his departure? Paul had always assumed him to be du Toit's right-hand man. Never Slug!

Du Toit didn't reply immediately. Only after they'd reached the top of the *koppie* did he stop and swing round to face Paul.

'Sometimes,' he said, 'people do things, say things, you don't expect. Being a captain isn't easy, hey!' He spread his arms wide to indicate the view, smiling wryly as he did so. 'It's lonely at the top.' Then, smile fading, he fastened his unfathomable gaze on Paul again and said, 'That's why I rely on you.'

Briefly, it seemed as if he might be about to step forward and touch Paul with a still-extended hand. Until, hand dropping, he turned away slightly and Paul was left feeling he might have dreamt the moment. 'Anyway, now you can see for yourself,' he continued quietly, eyes on the landscape, 'how hard it is to grow stuff here.'

From where they stood, Paul could also see how large the farm must once have been. And that the land ahead was in fact still being cultivated, presumably by whoever had bought it from the du Toits. Industrial-sized sprinklers had created squares of vivid green, stretching into the far distance, offsetting the prevailing brown.

Then he noticed a further source of water: a small dam at the foot of the *koppie*, near which, behind a bamboo fence, stood an arrangement of thatched rondavels, their terracotta walls showing signs of having once been painted in a series of geometric patterns.

'That's where our land stops now,' said du Toit, pointing. 'By the *kraal*.'

'So what does he actually do then, your dad,' ventured Paul, 'if he can't really farm any more?'

'Government mostly,' said du Toit enigmatically. 'Stuff for the government.'

'What kind of stuff?'

'What's it to you?'

'I'm only asking.'

'*Ag*, who cares about work? Work's boring. Does *your* dad talk about his?'

As it happened, Douglas did. Mealtimes were often taken up with stories of what had befallen people foolish enough not to have taken out insurance. But, if du Toit didn't want to talk about his own father's work, then, as with his absent mother, the topic must remain off limits.

Meanwhile, du Toit had broken into another trot, this time down the far side of the *koppie*, at the foot of which they came to the dam, its dark green waters throwing up a sudden stench of rotting vegetation.

'Where now?' asked Paul, wrinkling his nose.

'This way!' commanded du Toit, swerving on to a path with a friable skin of dried mud, along which they soon came to the bamboo fence that surrounded the huts Paul had seen from the top of the *koppie*. Here du Toit explained, 'We mustn't go into the hut unless he invites us. Okay? And don't ask any of your stupid questions. There isn't time. Also, it isn't polite.'

This, Paul decided, had to be where Tsebo lived. Whoever Tsebo was. Although, before he could ask even that, du Toit had slipped through a gap in the fence.

The ground inside the *kraal* was even drier and dustier than on the outside, yielding only some wilted weeds and a smattering of virtual junk: an old tin bowl or two, a sheet of corrugated iron, a roll of wire, some rickety chairs, on one of which, face to the sun, sat a frail old man. His few tight curls were completely grey, as was his sketchy beard, and a roughly hewn walking stick was propped against one thigh. All the same, he was not without majesty. His eyes, which had registered the arrival of the boys the minute they appeared through the fence, might have been rheumy but they were also keen; and against the shining blackness of his skin his white shirt blazed.

'You have brought a friend to see me,' he said as they approached. 'I like it very much to meet your friends.'

'*Dumela*,' said du Toit, dipping his head.

'What then is your name?' asked Tsebo, for this had to be Tsebo, looking at Paul.

'He's called Harvey,' said du Toit. 'We're in the same class.'

'I am pleased to meet you, Harvey,' said Tsebo, raising a hand. 'You must be a good friend to Andre if he brings you here. That makes me happy. A boy needs good friends. Is that not so, Andre?'

'Actually, Pa asked him,' said du Toit, 'if you must know. And anyway, it's only an exeat.' His head was still lowered, arms held smartly at his sides. 'Pa also says,' he went on, 'that he'll see you tomorrow. He had some calls to make and Harvey's parents are coming too.'

'Tell your father I am well today,' replied Tsebo. 'He must not to worry.' He looked again at Paul. 'Every Sunday,' he said, 'if I am not well, then Andre will visit me. He is very good.'

'But we've got to go,' interrupted du Toit. 'We can't be late for lunch.'

'Ah!' chuckled Tsebo, face breaking into a toothless smile. 'Or Violet will be cross. Tsebo knows! Shoosh!' He made a sucking sound. 'And when Violet is cross, life is difficult!' Placing both palms together, he effected a slight bow of his own. 'Be safe, my children, and return soon.'

'Come!' ordered du Toit, reaching out a hand again so that, for the first time ever, he actually touched Paul. Just a quick tug of the arm, to pull him away. 'Come!'

As the boys ran back along the path they'd already marked with their flashing sandals, then around the foul-smelling dam and over the *koppie*, Paul tried to make sense of the day so far. Du Toit's unexpected moments of warmth, bracketed by his usual coldness. The mystery of the mother. Disdainful Laura. Tsebo and his presumed wife, Violet, since that was who, from the way Tsebo had spoken of her, Paul imagined the as yet unmet Violet to be.

How exactly did this family, to whom he'd been given such unforeseen access, function? Because one thing was certain: the du Toits were not like the Harveys. And so his thoughts came round to Peggy and Douglas, whom he was missing, he realised, and had been all morning. Quite badly, truth be told. Of course he'd seen his mother at cricket yesterday, when it had been agreed that Mr du Toit would collect Paul in the morning and that the adult Harveys should come separately, around lunchtime, but not for long: she'd been talking too much to Mr du Toit. And anyway, it was only she who'd been there. Douglas had had some unexpected work to deal with in the office, apparently.

Du Toit rounded the last of the outbuildings and the stoep came into view again. On it Paul saw: a uniformed maid with a tray; Peggy in the same silly dress she'd worn to cricket yesterday; Douglas in his customary suit; while Mr du Toit, cigarette in mouth, commanded the steps.

'There you are!' he cried as the boys ran up. 'We were about to send out a search party. Hey, Peggy?'

'Hello, darling,' smiled Peggy, coming to stand alongside Mr du Toit. 'Don't you look hot! *Must* you always run?'

Her dress and the utter predictability of her greeting notwithstanding, Paul wanted only to hug her. But didn't dare. Not in that company. And besides, Mr du Toit precluded the possibility by clamping a firm hand on to his shoulder.

'I think you'll find,' he said, steering Paul away from Peggy and up the steps, 'that Violet has another something on her tray for you. Then after – okay, Andre, no arguing? – go and wash your hands and find Laura. Lunch'll be ready soon. *Ja*, Violet? *Is dit gereed?*'

The maid nodded, at the same time indicating with a twinkle very like Mosa's that Paul should help himself to more cooldrink from her tray. 'How is Tsebo?' she asked du Toit quietly as he did this.

The adults, by contrast, appeared – in true adult fashion – to have forgotten them already. Mr du Toit was repeating, sort of, what he'd said in the car that morning, while Peggy and Douglas were also explaining, but in a more muted manner, their story being less boastworthy, how they too had arrived in the Transvaal. What Britain had been like in the aftermath of the war. The cold. The rationing. The lack of opportunity. Future uncertain. Until eventually, thanks in part to a government scheme, they'd boarded the *Stirling Castle*. They spoke about their first, breathtaking sight of Table Mountain as their ship sailed into Cape Town harbour. The job that Douglas was coming to, in Johannesburg. Less breathtaking, but a good opportunity, all the same. Future more certain. Then being transferred to Pretoria and their concomitant move to Nellmapius. Paul's start at St Luke's.

'Such a pretty village!' exclaimed Mr du Toit. 'So English in its way. You must feel at home there.'

'Well,' said Peggy, 'to an extent, yes, I suppose we do.'

'But I can't believe there's any question! And I'm sure you're a real asset to the community. Am I right?'

There was for Paul, in the giggling way Peggy now patted her hair, something quite unlike her normal behaviour; something that echoed, or so he thought as he watched from the bench where he and du Toit had taken their cooldrinks, her frock. Which he knew he should have welcomed, having always wanted Peggy to dress more like the other mothers. But, now that she had, he was in fact finding that he didn't want it quite as much as he'd thought he did. The frock was too brightly patterned. And short. Way too short. Tight also. With a dress like that, you needed a tan.

And apparently Douglas thought likewise; well, if the look he was giving Peggy was anything to go by.

Then Mr du Toit cried, with a clap of his meaty hands, 'Ready, boys? I don't know about anyone else, but this *ou* could eat an ox.'

Du Toit rose from the bench and, with a quick, impatient glance at Paul, took his empty glass back to the tray Violet had left on a nearby table before running towards the door through which Laura had vanished earlier.

'Honestly, I give up!' Paul heard his mother murmur with another giggle as he dashed after him. 'The way these boys carry on! Always running, never walking. Hormones, do you think?'

Despite similarities of layout, the du Toits' house appeared more spacious than the Nellmapius one. Where the Harveys tended to live compactly, there was a sense of leeway here, of unconstraint – more rooms than were strictly necessary for just a father, son and daughter with no apparent mother; more furniture in those rooms too, from what Paul could see as they ran past their often open doors. And, on the dun passage walls, ranks of black and white photographs. Generations of dour du Toits, it would seem, all in their Sunday best and facing up to the camera as if for the Day of Judgement.

Laura's room, its door closed, was at the far end of the passage. Though a closed door wasn't any impediment to du Toit, not du Toit, who barged in without knocking to announce, 'Lunch is ready!'

His sister had changed out of her uniform and was standing by the window in a simple dress of blue that, while nicely matching the colour of her eyes, didn't begin to take into account the expression there: full-on fury that her brother hadn't knocked.

'Who the hell do you think you are, hey?' she demanded. 'Little pig!'

'Well, are you coming or aren't you?' replied an unfazed du Toit. 'Pa's waiting, and you don't want to make him *voes*.'

Then he turned to run back down the passage and Laura transferred her gaze to Paul, holding him captive briefly with the overt curiosity in her look. Combined with his own curiosity, of course, as to what it might be like to have a sibling, something he'd often pondered.

Would life be different – less lonely? easier? happier? – with a sister or brother to share it with?

'Is he being nice to you?' she asked. 'You must say if he isn't.' Then, 'But what are you waiting for, hey? *I'm* not in charge of you. Lunch *is* ready, *ja*? That's what he said, isn't it?'

The dining room, when Paul finally reached it, having stopped along the way to wash his hands, reminded him of the Harveys' own. It too was gloomy, its furniture equally severe, though, where the Harveys' table and chairs were of oak, the du Toits' were of some very dark wood, almost black in places, heavy and extremely old-fashioned-looking. Rather like the family photographs, more of which hung in judgement here as well.

Paul's parents were already seated, one on each side of Mr du Toit, who'd claimed the head of the table and who now indicated to Paul where he should sit, which was opposite his son. The chair at the far end was intended, it seemed, for Laura, of whom Mr du Toit asked testily, 'Why's *she* being a slowcoach now?' And, when she did appear, 'At this rate, Laura, the food'll be cold, hey, and you'll owe Violet an apology.' He lowered his head and said solemnly, '*Seën Here hierdie voedsel en die hande wat dit voorberei het en maak ons opreg dankbaar daarvoor. Amen.*'

Grace over, Violet, who'd been hovering like Mosa alongside an elaborately carved dresser, began ladling food on to the plates she had there: a mince dish of some sort, with vegetables coming separately from dishes set on the table.

Five

'That's right!' instructed Mr du Toit as Violet began serving the plates. 'Dig in, everyone. Help yourselves. Don't hold back.'

'Smells delicious,' said Peggy. 'What is it?'

'*Bobotie*,' said Mr du Toit, going on to explain how the dish had originally been brought to the Cape by Malay slaves 'way back when'.

Not that Paul was listening. Rather, he was concentrating on the person opposite, trying to infer from du Toit's expression how he himself should be reacting. Would an exaggerated rolling of the eyes at the oddness of adults be in order? Or a shared giggle at something amusing? Or was boredom more appropriate? And was Laura to be included in whatever they did decide to communicate to each other, or should they simply be ignoring her, as she was them?

Simultaneously, the adults were talking history: history and its inevitable adjunct, politics. Having extolled at some length the glories of South Africa – why it was that people had always been drawn here from the Cape's earliest days – Mr du Toit went on to warn against elements that lurked beneath the beguiling surface: elements to be wary of, he said, if you wanted to stay out of trouble. Of course, he didn't mean to suggest that a person must worry, as he knew some people had after Sharpeville. That wasn't his point at all; that kind of thing was under control now, well under control. No, it was just that, in a country like South Africa, it was wise to keep your eyes peeled, that was all.

'So tell me,' murmured Laura, looking at Paul, 'what's he like at school? As popular as he pretends?'

Aware of du Toit's cool gaze on him also, Paul said, '*Ja*, everyone wants to be his friend.'

'Everyone?'

'But not everyone can be.'

'Why?'

'Because of how his club works.'

'Club? What club?'

Du Toit interrupted with, 'I'm not sure Barnabas really knows what he's talking about.'

'Barnabas?' queried Laura. 'Who's Barnabas?'

But here Paul, having taken heed of the warning, somehow managed to change the subject while at the same time Mr du Toit was saying, 'You will of course have heard the weekend news. About this Helen Joseph woman being put under house arrest. First person ever, but if we didn't have such laws, how the hell, hey, are these people to be stopped? Because they tried to charge her before, you know, but she got off. Like that Mandela fellow, last time round. The courts can't always be trusted. But, as it is, she won't be leaving her house again in a hurry, our Mrs Joseph, that's for sure.'

Then in bustled Violet with dessert.

'Pineapple fritters, *baas* Andre, your favourite!' she said with a smile, setting the plate down in the centre of the table.

Laura and her father also broke into smiles.

'*Sal ons tweede kom, dan*?' asked Mr du Toit.

'Pa!' said du Toit warningly.

'I don't feel like coming second today,' smirked Laura. 'I'd rather come first.'

'Laura!' Du Toit was beginning to sound really fussed.

'I don't get it,' said Paul.

'Andre,' explained Mr du Toit, still smiling, 'when he was younger, this is, said one day at dinner – we were also having fritters – that he wanted to come second. None of us had a clue what he meant. Then his mother worked it out. Seconds! He wanted seconds.'

Violet, who'd finished placing dessert bowls in front of everyone, asked softly, '*Koffie, baas?*'

'*Ja,*' said Mr du Toit. '*Asseblief*. But on the stoep, okay.' Adding, once she'd withdrawn, the same exhortation as at the start of the meal: 'Dig in everyone. Help yourselves. Don't hold back.'

Well, well – who would have thought! Paul found he was smiling too, inwardly at least, as he speared himself a fritter. *Sal ons tweede kom*? A handy deterrent against further use of his hated third Christian name.

'Another of our specialties, this,' Mr du Toit was saying as he too took a fritter. 'Or do you get them in England also?'

'No,' said Peggy. 'I don't think we do, actually.'

'What puddings do you have, you poms?'

'Well,' said Peggy, 'Paul's favourite – isn't it, dear? – is Queen of Puddings.'

'Queen of Puddings?' echoed Mr du Toit with a snort. 'That's funny. Very royal.'

'Moreish, though,' said Peggy. 'We had it last Sunday, didn't we, darling?'

'Ah!' said Mr du Toit. 'Of course. The priest. And the priest's son. What's his name again? Simon, is it?'

And so, as they tackled their steaming fritters – which had to be eaten with care, Paul discovered, otherwise you could scald your tongue on the hot fruit encased within the batter – the talk turned to the Tindalls, about whom Mr du Toit wanted to know everything, down to the last detail.

After lunch, the adults repaired to the stoep, Laura to her room and du Toit asked, as he and Paul also left the dining room, 'What now?'

'Your dad doesn't make you rest?'

'Why would he do that? I'm not a baby. We can either play in my room or go outside.'

'It'll be hot outside.'

'Okay, so my room, then. I'll catch you there. I need the toilet.'

Then off he zoomed without explaining where 'there' was, abandoning Paul to the unsmiling eyes of the du Toit in the photograph opposite. The man wore a dark coat that buttoned to the neck and, above that, a bushy beard which grew only beneath and around the man's chin, the Transvaal fashion back then. Why, Paul couldn't imagine; it looked plain silly.

But enough of ancestors! He was here to spend time with a living du Toit and so, turning from the photograph, he started in the direction of Laura's room, which was where, he reckoned, du Toit's own must be. At that end of the house, certainly.

The first room he passed had a piano in it and some tall glass cabinets against one wall, in which he could see sheets of music and some other, smaller musical instruments: a violin, a ukulele, a couple of recorders.

Next came a study containing a vast desk made of the same dark wood as the dining room table. On it were laid some papers, neatly stacked; no chaos here. And on the walls, as if there weren't enough of them elsewhere, more photos, one of which caused him to step gingerly forward. It was of a younger du Toit, standing in front of his father and a woman whose warm smile and cocked head was at pleasing variance with the stiffness on display everywhere else. A light hand rested on du Toit's shoulder. His mother, presumably. Who looked nice. Really nice.

Then something else caught Paul's attention. On top of the neatly stacked papers lay the object he'd so painstakingly pilfered from Spier. The wooden comb, or whatever it was. In plain sight.

A swirl of questions, suppositions, wild imaginings gripped hold of him as he stared, open-mouthed, at what he'd stumbled across. It was like an earthquake, bringing different parts of his life, of himself, into violent contact with each other. Then, deciding at last that his only course of action was to make sure du Toit didn't discover what he now knew, he quickly withdrew and continued along the passage, eventually coming upon the room he'd been in search of. He knew because on the bookcase was a collection of comics, which he at once, and avidly, began to leaf through, finding *Boy's Own*; *Eagle*, which had Dan Dare in it; and, best of all, *Beano*: Dennis the Menace, the Bash Street Kids, Roger the Dodger. For a boy confined to *Classics Illustrated*, these could almost take care of – well, for a while at least – the memory of what he'd just seen lying on Mr du Toit's well-ordered desk.

'He hasn't left you alone, has he?' came a voice. 'He really should know better.'

Looking up, Paul's startled eyes encountered those of Laura, who stood framed in the doorway: a living rather than a photographic portrait; full-length, too.

'He's in the toilet,' he explained, 'that's all.'

'Still,' she said, coming forward. 'He can be very rude.' She leaned nonchalantly against the cupboard. 'How long has it been now?'

'What?'

'That you've been friends. He hasn't mentioned you before, see.'

'Well,' replied Paul, relinquishing the comic he'd been poring over, 'I only joined his club last week.'

'*Ja*, and this club of his. Tell me, is it—?'

But she got no further. Du Toit had returned and was scowling ferociously at the interloper.

'Who gave you permission?' he demanded. 'And anyway, whose guest is he, hey?'

'Yours, of course,' Laura retorted, raising a tanned arm, strong and supple-looking, to brush a hair from her face. 'So don't go leaving him alone. Behave, Andre. Like *Ma* would want. This isn't polite, what you're doing.'

'Says who?'

'Says me!'

Brother and sister glared at each other. Then, glancing at Paul for a further second with a wholly sympathetic look, Laura slipped away.

Five

'*Blerrie* busybody,' spat du Toit, throwing himself on to the bed. 'She never knows when to keep out of other people's beeswax. You're *blerrie* lucky not having a sister. You haven't, have you? And I bet your pa doesn't act like mine does either. Trying to humiliate you in front of your friends.'

'You mean about the seconds? He was only teasing, wasn't he?'

'You think you can trust them,' said du Toit darkly. 'But you can't. I really hate him. *And* her. They're always ganging up on me. *Blerrie* family!'

Paul thought of all the photos on the wall. And of his own, much smaller and more distant family circle – in particular, the grandmother who'd only come to visit once but who wrote to him constantly nonetheless and who'd also, of course, given him his diary. Which made him wonder whether, since he'd never experienced du Toit in a vulnerable mood before, this might not be the moment to ask why, if du Toit didn't like being ganged up on himself, he'd thought it acceptable to gang up on Paul by stealing his diary?

Or: what about du Toit's mother? He could ask again about her. Or the club. Lombard's dismissal. Slug's position within it. Even what he'd seen on Mr du Toit's desk. He could even do that.

Except du Toit, having by now recovered, was asking a question of his own.

'What did you tell her, anyway? About the club? And don't pretend you didn't. I heard her asking.'

'Nothing. Promise!'

'Cross your heart? 'Cause if you want to stay I have to be able to trust you. You mustn't talk about it to other people. Not ever. Got that?'

Numbly, Paul nodded.

'So how many Dinky toys have *you* got, then?' came next. 'Want to check out mine?' And, so saying, he threw open his cupboard to reveal a collection of miniature cars that easily outstripped, in terms of number and variety, the comics. Whatever else might be lacking in du Toit's life, it wasn't toys.

Lifting out a sleek blue car with tapering tail fins, a beige roof and an answering strip of beige along its sides, he said with a fierce grin, 'DeSoto Fireflite. Got it in the holidays. Tit, hey?'

I also remember, from that fateful day, walking back down the passage after we'd finished playing with du Toit's Dinky toys and how ashamed I felt in passing, for a second time, Mr du Toit's study: ashamed that I'd somehow betrayed Spier, who'd always been so kind to me.

I remember that Violet had set out more cooldrink for us on the stoep, and that the adults drank tea. My relief that we weren't expected, as I would have been at home, to eat anything more than another rusk.

I remember that at one point Tsebo was mentioned again, because that was when I learned that he'd had an operation of some sort. And how Violet, who was still present, started chuckling in the background: 'Lazy! That man is just too, too lazy.'

Though when it comes to female behaviour it's my mother who stands out. How she would throw back her head when she laughed; as if on-stage, under the spotlight. How she would run a graceful hand through the luxuriance of her hair. While my largely silent father just watched; watched intently.

I remember too that when it was time to leave, because Laura had to be returned to school as well, it was decided that, if Mr du Toit drove her, my parents could then take du Toit and myself. To save Mr du Toit unnecessary mileage.

I can also recall, as we stood under the blue gum where the cars were parked, how, with smoke curling from him again, another cigarette, the hairs on the back of Mr du Toit's hand seemed to catch fire in the sun as he extended it to shake my own goodbye.

With, this time, my mother as the watcher.

And in the car, dirt road becoming tar, veld becoming suburb, how Peggy attempted to find out, with some gentle probing, what the story was with du Toit's own mother.

Douglas saying, 'Peggy, leave it.'

And, 'Sometimes I wonder at you, really I do.'

Then parking in the school driveway, my parents thanking du Toit for a lovely day, and the way in which he ran off, as if glad to be shot of us. My mother giving me, from the boot, a tin of tuck for the coming week as she kissed me farewell.

And how, once I'd made my own dash for the steps, I paused for a moment to look back at them. A last wave; it was our custom. The sight of them standing side by side before their modest Cortina, my mother in that dress, and how a separate image superimposed itself on that of Peggy and Douglas by the car: Peggy and Mr du Toit after she'd come to stand beside him on the steps of the farm stoep when du Toit and I ran up to them.

Her saying, 'Don't you look hot!'

When actually, the flushed one was her.

Six

PAUL WAS in the pavilion, pairing cricket pads, a job he often got given after games. The masters knew he wouldn't protest at having to check that the number written on the back of each pad matched that of the pad it accompanied before then stowing them, having also checked none was missing, in their allocated locker. He was unremittingly reliable when it came to tasks like this. All the masters said so.

Also in the locker were the batsmen's boxes, which for some reason he couldn't yet articulate held a strange fascination for Paul. And indeed, he was about to lift one up in order to run an illicit, thrilled finger over its moulded contours when he heard his name being called.

Spinning round, he saw Slug peering in through the open doorway.

'What now?' he snapped.

'Club meeting,' said Slug, advancing. 'It's taken me ages to find you. What are you doing? I haven't caught you out, have I?'

Stepping back from the telltale locker, Paul said, 'None of your beeswax.' Adding just as sharply, in case Slug didn't get the point, 'Got that?'

Usually, when chastised, Slug would accept any ticking-off without demur. Today, however, he just came closer, magnified eyes staying on Paul as he said, 'Sorry. I didn't mean to upset you, Harvey.'

He appeared to be not just offering an apology, but making some sort of overture. Of potential friendship, perhaps? Now they were both club members? But Paul was not inclined to play ball.

'It's okay, I'm finished,' he said, voice still sharp. 'We can go if you want.'

They left the pavilion in silence and it was some moments before Slug dared ask, as they trotted towards the school boundary, 'What's it actually like on the farm? Does he really have so many Dinky toys? And his sister? Is she really tit?'

This surprised Paul. 'He says that?'

Slug nodded. 'And clever, he says, and kind. They're really close, he says. You must have heard him.'

'What else does he say?'

'About his sister?'

'I was thinking more his mum. Has he ever talked about her?'

Slug pushed his glasses, which had a tendency to slip down the pink blob that was his nose, back into place as he considered the question. Then he said, but cautiously, 'Why, has something happened?'

But if Slug didn't know, Paul wasn't about to enlighten him. And anyway, what would he say, knowing next to nothing himself? Nor did he intend to tell Slug about the farm, even though he could tell how desperate Slug was for information.

'Never mind,' he said. 'It's nothing.'

To which Slug, who was by now panting slightly, replied, 'You don't know how lucky you are. Lombard was asked, when he was number one. A couple of times. So why not me? Why you and not me?' Adding, as an afterthought, 'You don't think you could ask him for me, do you? I'd pay you back.'

'Really? How?'

'With some of my tuck, if you like. I know how little pocket money you get.'

But if Slug imagined this would aid his case he couldn't have been more mistaken. To comment on a person's pocket money was tantamount to insulting their parents; only the feeblest would stand for it. And with Slug of all people Paul didn't intend to be feeble!

'Ask someone else,' he said, speeding up so as to outrun slightly his wheezy companion, 'if you have to. I'm not your servant.'

A cluster of juniors looked up, meerkat-like, as the two of them now dropped into the ditch. Then disappeared, giggling, into their own hut while Slug solemnly knocked on the door of a more desired establishment. (Knock) 'I …' (knock) '… ask …' (knock) '… permission.' (knock).

The meeting that followed was similar to Paul's first in other respects too. Again the others were already present as he and Slug ducked inside the hut; there was the same smell of damp, decaying earth, the same gloom, and, on his throne, with the same plastic helmet on his head, the stern, unsmiling figure of their captain.

Slug took up his clipboard. There was a seemingly unnecessary (and again embarrassing) roll-call, the minutes, then a short speech from the captain. A most gratifying speech, too, as far as Paul was concerned. Last week he'd stood at number four. This week, thanks to his successful task, he found himself at number three. One above Horton.

'That's not fair!'

The objection came, unsurprisingly, from the new number four.

'Excuse me?' The icy response was the captain's.

In the ensuing hush, heads were lowered, eyes averted and for what seemed like an age all Paul could hear was some muffled giggling from the neighbouring juniors.

Then du Toit said, into the hush, 'Murray, ask Horton what his problem is.'

Slug obliged with, 'What's the problem, Horton?'

Horton said, 'We still don't know what Harvey had to do.'

Then another pause, broken by the right-hand man concurring. 'He's right, captain. Last meeting, I did say—'

But du Toit cut him short. 'If I decide a task must be secret, then that's how it stays. Okay? Got that?'

Paul still had his eyes on the ground. Nevertheless, he could physically feel du Toit looking from one to the other of them; slowly; intently; commandingly. 'What are we?' he asked eventually.

They immediately chorused, 'Your club!'

'What do we do?'

'Work together!'

'Who do we fear?'

'No one!'

'And who do we follow?'

'You, captain!'

Satisfied, the captain announced that at some stage it would be necessary for Horton to undertake a new task, yet to be decided. No other tasks were specified, though Slug did remind him that he'd promised they would one day mount an expedition against the nearby juniors because, it was suspected, one or more of their number had presumed to go into their hut when no one was there.

Then it was dismissal time.

Outside, it was dusk already, the sky having turned from its usual faraway blue to something inkier and closer-seeming as the earth was swaddled for the night in darkness. A glint of metal impinged itself on Paul's consciousness: Horton's saliva-strung braces.

'I'll find out,' he whispered furiously, freckled face thrust into Paul's. 'And if it isn't something really hard, hey, you won't have heard the last of it. Secret! Huh! Why does yours have to be so secret!' Then he fell away and another face orbited into view, eyes a cool, calculating echo of the colour the sky no longer was.

'You mustn't worry about them,' said du Toit, matching his steps to Paul's. 'They'll soon forget. You just keep on looking. And in fact, why don't you bring your diary back into school? I won't touch it this time, promise, then you can use it to keep a proper log of what you see or find. For your report. *Ja*?'

'Tell me,' said Paul, judging the moment to have arrived at last. 'Why did you do it?'

'What?'

'Steal it, of course.'

'*Ag*, it was only for a few days, man.'

'I know that. And?'

'So okay.' Du Toit paused. 'It's like Spier is always saying: we shouldn't think we're better than other people.'

This threw Paul utterly. 'Just because I keep a diary,' he queried, 'I think I'm better?'

'Well, it makes you different, that's for sure,' said du Toit. 'Who else keeps a diary? And all right, I admit, I was curious.'

'How much did you read?'

'Enough to know you could do with some help.'

'Help? Me? Why?' Though naturally he could guess.

'Don't be dim, Harvey. Where were you born?'

'Here, of course.'

'So this is where you belong, hey? You mustn't always be wondering about other places. Which aren't any better, anyway. If you think about it, they're often worse. North Vietnam. Cuba. Like I say, I was only trying to help.'

That night, after lights-out, Paul stared and stared at his usual oblong of sky. Sometimes, while doing this, the stars would grant him a sort of release, their very distance and obvious indifference allowing him to put his own concerns into perspective. Tonight, however, the world felt not only unheeding, but ultimately unknowable. As much of a mystery as the doings of a du Toit. Quite beyond the comprehension of a mere Harvey.

He turned on to his side and began concentrating instead on another formula for making himself feel better when he couldn't sleep, which was to covertly rule for a while over the kingdom he imagined for himself on his bed: the counterpane hills and valleys of a miniature world, peopled by ant-like beings over whom, as their sole monarch, wearing an imaginary robe of rich velvet and carrying an imaginary sceptre shaped much like a cricket box, he had complete control.

'*Omphaloskepsis*,' said Spier, raking the semi-circle of boys before him with those searching brown eyes of his. 'Anyone?'

Predictably, the challenge was met by six blank stares. Being members of a general knowledge club did not mean they could therefore grasp ancient Greek; or even that this *was* ancient Greek.

'Right!' said Spier. '*Omphalos*, meaning navel. *Skepsis*, the act of looking. Together you get?'

'To look at your navel, sir?' volunteered Lombard.

'Not the literal meaning, Lombard,' groaned Spier. 'I've just given you that. Something more general. Metaphorical, if you like.'

The stares remained blank.

'Okay, so I'm going to read to you from Monday's paper,' he continued, rummaging on his desk for a copy of the *Pretoria News*, which he held aloft with the headlines facing them. 'Monday's edition, on the front page no less, at the bottom there. *FUDGE, OUR CAT, HAS GONE – AND KITTENS WAIT.*'

'Oh, yes, sir, please, sir,' said Bentley major. 'Fudge is famous. Ma says the paper writes about her all the time, ever since she had her kittens under a reporter's desk. But you must know, sir, you read it too.'

'Perhaps,' said Spier drily, 'I prefer *my* news more wide-ranging. But anyway…' Settling himself against his desk, he slapped the paper straight, cleared his throat and began to read: *Missing – our cat Fudge. Mewlingly mourned by her five kittens, whose experience of this sorry world now includes some knowledge of the pangs of hunger. Fudge, Pretoria's most publicised cat, was last seen at 11.27 on Saturday night. Next morning, about 11am, a sub-editor came to the office on a mission of mercy – with a parcel of raw fish for her. Fudge was nowhere to be seen, so he put the fish in the usual place and went away. About 5.30pm when he returned, he found the fish untouched, and the five kittens mewing with hunger. When a woman telex operator came in to sort out the copy flowing from the machines, she went into action with a teaspoon to feed the kittens artificially. She took them home with her – and frequently during the night she rose to feed them. This morning the motherless mewlers had their first taste of mincemeat – and liked it. What happened to Fudge? Was she killed by a passing car? No, said the municipality's "dead animals" department. Not a single cat was a road casualty in Pretoria at the weekend. The SPCA's Col. J.C. Mooiman assured us that she wasn't there. He also gave instructions on how to feed and rear the kittens. What happened to her? Is she locked in a cupboard somewhere? Strayed or stolen? No one knows. But if she is still alive, she must be in pain by now because of the accumulation of milk. General feeling among the staff is that the cat is seeking publicity again – and will turn up during the course of the day with a smug, self-satisfied gleam in her eye and a fish-head in her mouth.'*

Having finished, he held the paper aloft again, at the same time pointing to the main headline: *SABOTEURS STRIKE IN SIX PLACES*.

Next to it was a second headline, which he also indicated: *MANDELA TRIAL POSTPONED FOR A WEEK*.

Between the two headlines were a couple of photos, the first of a police-cordoned crowd, the second of a young black woman wearing a tribal headdress and masses of bead jewellery strung tightly about her neck.

'So!' said Spier, tossing the paper aside. 'In a week when we went so far as to put our first citizen under house arrest and the trial of Mr Mandela also started (before it got postponed, that is), with such a crowd gathering outside the courthouse – in spite of its being held here in Pretoria – that a police presence was required, and when his wife, like her husband, in order to snub the authorities, came in tribal dress – that's her in the photo, in case you're wondering – what does the *Pretoria News* put on its front page? Fudge the cat! Therefore I repeat: *omphaloskepsis*. Anyone care to try now?'

'Are you saying, sir,' said Bentley major, 'that we shouldn't care about Fudge? Wouldn't that be cruel?'

'Those kittens will be just fine,' said Spier, starting to pace. 'They've an entire newspaper organisation – an entire city – worrying about them. So if we are going to think about hunger, which I do agree is an issue, how about the thousands of black children who, according to recent statistics, are starving to death? Actually starving.' He looked assiduously at each of them in turn. 'Which of you knows,' he asked, 'how much, more or less, the average mine worker earns? Black mine worker, I mean.'

Again there was silence.

'Eight rand a week is not unknown. While a white miner, admittedly with a qualification, can earn ten times as much. More to the point – no? – than kittens.' He stopped his pacing in order to lean once more against the edge of his desk. 'Or how about looking at the concept of arrest. What does the word mean? Arrest.'

Lombard said confidently, 'To lock someone up, sir.'

'And that implies?'

Behind his glasses, Lombard began to look uncertain. 'Sir?'

'If you arrest someone, what does that usually mean?'

'That you put them in jail, sir,' said Bentley major, coming to Lombard's rescue.

'Exactly!' cried Spier. 'So – is a house an obvious jail?'

'No, sir,' interjected Horton. 'A house is where you live. You don't have cells in a house, or prison warders or electric fences or lookout posts or searchlights or anything.' It was with some relish that he listed all the characteristics of prison he could think of.

'So is it right,' Spier said, 'to keep someone under lock and key in their own home? Or is that a perversion of justice? And are there other ways, too, of wrongly imprisoning a person? For instance, can we ever become our own jailors, would you say? Can we be tricked into locking ourselves up and throwing away the key simply by not doing or saying things that we know other people might not want us to do or say?'

He stared hard at the members of his General Knowledge Club.

Again, I wonder: did he really did say all this? Or am I, more than usually because of what I know now, putting words into his mouth? Though during that session he was certainly less than oblique, confrontational almost – that, I do most distinctly remember. But this is about the sum of it, if I'm honest, since young Paul wasn't really paying attention. How could he? He had other concerns. Like: how would he look for something on Spier's desk today? Without letting the gnawing unease he still felt at being such a spy, at betraying Spier's trust, hamper him? Could the comb-like object be improved upon, and, with it, his ranking therefore in that other club to which he also now belonged?

In the meantime, they had progressed to, of all things, the weather. It was rumoured that given yesterday's temperature – a stonking 94.3 degrees in the shade, said the paper – summer could well turn out to be more than usually baking. Strover worried at the effect this might have on the pitch, Bentley major that the city's Jacaranda trees, already in purple bloom, hence the school colour, might lose their blossoms early, while du Toit maintained they should worry more about the Free State, where, or so his pa had said, there was such bad drought that farmers literally didn't know whether or not they would survive. *There* was potential hunger for you!

Hunger figured in another context as well: that of looming supper, heralded, of course, by Lombard.

As before, Paul didn't join the general stampede for the door, managing instead to go quite slowly past Spier's desk – or as slowly, at any rate, as he dared in the absence of assistance from du Toit, who on this occasion had, like usual, spearheaded the stampede. Surreptitiously, he scanned the customary jumble of newspapers, pens, pencils, rubber bands and such, the piles of exercise books; and, poking out from under these, the small black book Spier used for keeping track of borrowings. Would this be worth taking? Yes, why not! Though, as he glanced up to make sure he wasn't being observed, he found to his horror that the others had left already, leaving him hopelessly exposed.

'Come on, Harvey!' chided Spier from where he stood by the open door. 'Not hungry too?'

Keeping his head down, Paul sped obediently towards the beckoning master, who, although he tended to notice when you became nervous, did little more today than pat Paul on the shoulder as he scuttled past.

Phew!

Relieved to be out in the open, even if in the end he'd left without achieving anything, Paul ran in a sort of daze towards the main building, trying not to dwell on his failure. There would be time enough later, he told himself, for more information-gathering, more stealing. He wasn't at all sure where, or how, but still, unless he wanted to drive himself mad, he had to believe that somehow, somewhere, it would prove possible.

And indeed, it very shortly would. Though not in any way he could have predicted.

The next afternoon, after games, the boys were allowed, in two batches, juniors first, seniors second, to use the pool. Paul therefore took his towel and costume with him to cricket so that afterwards he could head straight for his swim. Botma was in charge and, as he signalled the end of their game, which he did by sidling towards where he'd slung his jacket over the wicket in order to retrieve from it his matches and pipe, Paul ran from his position mid-field to where, by the boundary, he'd left his rolled-up towel. As he did so, he heard a warning shout. 'Duck, man, quick!'

Labuschagne, who'd been bowling, must have wanted to send one final ball Horton's way; and Horton must have then hit the ball in Paul's direction. Or so Paul could only surmise as instinctively he dived sideways, tripping in the process on a length of string pegged tautly along the boundary line. Pheko's doing, for during their game the crouching groundsman had been giving the side-lines a fresh coat of white paint.

Elbow first, Paul hit the ground hard. Nearby, the ball did likewise; Paul heard the thwack of it, followed by a ripple of distant laughter. Then footsteps and he was staring into a pair of dark and unfamiliar eyes.

'Is the *baas* hurt?' asked the young groundsman, though without of course seeking to help Paul up, as a teacher might have done.

'I'm fine,' said Paul. 'Really.'

Scrambling to his feet, he brushed with attempted unconcern at his dirtied shorts, ignoring the fact that his elbow, which he didn't inspect, was beginning to sting.

'But the *baas* is bleeding,' said Pheko. 'Here!' From the pocket of his own shorts he produced a handkerchief that was, unlike the rest of his attire, spotless – the same brilliant white indeed as the shirt of the old man called Tsebo.

Remembering Tsebo and how du Toit had behaved towards him during their exeat (with such surprising courtesy), Paul hesitated slightly before declining Pheko's offer. As he felt he must. Help from a servant – it could only lead to ridicule and too many people were watching. Just a curt shake of the head; that was all he managed.

The young groundsman had noted his hesitation, however, and with the merest smile simply let the handkerchief drop, forcing Paul to grab hold of it.

'The *baas* can give it back any time,' he said. 'The *baas* must not hurry.'

Avoiding as best he could the groundsman's continuing gaze, Paul began to dab at his elbow – which was bleeding quite profusely, he now saw – intending to hand the handkerchief back the minute he was done. Except that, by the time he'd staunched the blood, Pheko had returned to his line-painting and was a way off. So Paul just put the handkerchief into his pocket. He'd give it back later, he decided, when no one was around to mock and he could endeavour a proper thank-you.

Then, scooping up his swimming things, he made for the sound of splashing juniors.

The pool was a large one: virtually Olympic in size, according to Strover, who not surprisingly knew its every dimension. It had two diving boards, one high, one low, some stepped concrete benches along one edge of it and, beyond this rough provision for spectators, a spacious changing room. In charge that afternoon was Miss de Villiers, the art mistress, reclined like a film star under the *klieg* light of the late afternoon sun on one of the concrete benches. Seeing Paul, she sat up, consulted her diamanté-encrusted watch to check that it was time already for seniors, then waved him towards the changing room while simultaneously instructing the splashing juniors to finish up.

There were wooden benches against all four of the changing room's stockaded sides; also lines of regularly placed, eye-level metal hooks for hanging your clothes and towels upon. Paul went to the furthest of these – he preferred, if possible, to be near the corner in such circumstances – and began changing into his swimming costume.

Some breathless juniors entered, the same lot he and Slug had encountered outside du Toit's hut on Tuesday;

although now, as then, they steered clear of him, the only senior present, by scampering towards a section of bench well away from Paul's.

He was able, as a result, to continue undressing without having to take much notice of his surroundings, and was in the act of pulling tight the drawstring of his costume when, all of a sudden, he heard a familiar voice saying, 'So tell me, McCumskey, how's the water? Not too cold?'

Spier had appeared alongside the juniors, shirt half off already.

'No, sir, just right, sir,' said McCumskey.

'Good,' said Spier. 'That's what I like to hear.'

He seemed not to have noticed Paul – or, if he had, wasn't saying – which meant that Paul was able to watch quite blatantly as Spier undressed: shirt first; then his watch, which he put into a trouser pocket; then his shoes and socks; his trousers; and, finally, a pair of tight underpants, white like Pheko's handkerchief or Tsebo's shirt, take your pick.

Naked, Spier's body was a version of what Miss de Villiers sometimes pinned to her noticeboard in postcard form when wanting the class to consider the art of ancient Greece or Rome. Perfectly sculpted, in other words; but sculpted in flesh, living flesh, flesh which, except for the one area to which Paul felt his gaze being drawn, was quite tanned and, in places – that one place particularly – shockingly hairy. Unlike the postcards.

Paul's stomach went into freefall. Then everything stopped, the entire world, it just fell away, along with his

Six

stomach, leaving only him and Spier inside the stockaded changing room and himself unable to move until, at last, Spier pulled a flimsy triangle of black nylon over that part of himself Paul couldn't help staring at.

'Been in yet, Harvey?' asked the master as he stepped away from the bench, towel in one hand.

'No, sir,' managed Paul.

'After you, then,' said Spier, ushering Paul forward. 'Don't let me hold you back.'

Had he noticed Paul staring? Nothing indicated that he had; but there again, neither had his tone of voice, always somewhat teasing, precluded the possibility. Meanwhile, Paul's whole body (not just his elbow) had started to sting; or not sting, exactly, it was more that his skin felt unusually tight, as though trying to squeeze him into a new shape, and it was as much as he could do to run ahead of the master into the sparkling waters of the pool.

Over the next quarter of an hour or so, which was how long Spier stayed around, Paul remained acutely aware of the master's presence. First, Spier paused to talk to Miss de Villiers, who sat up eagerly as he came out of the changing room. Then he ascended the higher of the two boards and executed a faultless dive. He swam a few swift, churning lengths; then, while drying himself, returned to Miss de Villiers, who, as she listened to whatever he was saying, looked more conscious than ever of her putative star status: she held her head just so, kept fingering her stylish sunglasses, also her coiffed hair. It reminded Paul of something. What, though? Of course! His mother, and the way *she'd* behaved when talking to Mr du Toit.

Then finally Spier dematerialised and other claims began to be made on Paul's attention. More seniors had arrived by now, there was much good-natured shouting and splashing, and Lombard, who'd swum up to Paul, was saying, 'If you want, Harvey—'

But here Horton dive-bombed the pair of them, causing Miss de Villiers to call, 'Use the board, Horton, if you must dive! And just ten more minutes, everyone. Then it's time, I'm afraid.'

Lombard's head remained close, bobbing in the choppy water. Seemingly, he still intended to tell Paul whatever Horton had interrupted. Something to do, perhaps, with why he'd been chucked out of du Toit's club. For what else would Lombard, who wasn't a friend, want with Paul? But Paul didn't fancy staying in the pool any longer. What had happened to him earlier in the changing room was too much with him still, making him worry that something in his manner might betray the turmoil he was experiencing. So, despite his curiosity, he struck out for the side and was back in the changing room, wriggling out of his wet costume, well ahead of anyone else.

Dressed, he left the pool enclosure as fast as he could, deciding that now might be the moment to return Pheko's handkerchief, since everyone else was either swimming or drifting about the playground.

From the edge of the playing fields, he scanned their deserted expanse for a sign of his Good Samaritan.

Seeing nothing, at first, but green.

Then, in the distance, on the far side of the furthest field, a patch of khaki: his quarry, still line-painting.

Paul started in that direction, but hadn't gone far when he noticed something else: Spier, emerging from the masters' compound. On his way to supper duty perhaps. Except that no sooner had he reached the edge of the field where Pheko was working than he stopped. For a moment, he appeared not to move. Then he turned and walked back in the direction from which he'd come. Meanwhile, the crouching Pheko had risen to his feet and was looking swiftly – almost furtively – about him before also vanishing into the masters' compound.

What precisely this meant, Paul couldn't begin to guess at. But he did know this: he'd just witnessed a little something which might be used for his next task. Which could, in the absence of anything more tangible, form the crux of his report.

In my memory of these things, summer afternoon thunderstorms on the highveld used to be entirely, but entirely regular. One minute the sky was cloudless and were you to think of thunderheads at all it would have been in the abstract, their actuality seeming as remote as the sky was blue. Yet by mid-afternoon, like clockwork, the clouds would boil up, instilling a mixture of awe and respect, before retreating again in a series of diminishing rumbles until the morrow.

So, too, with the headmaster – although in Mr Wilson's case his fear-inducing appearances happened all year round and at morning assembly. Back ramrod-straight, leonine head held high, there he would stand on the stage, his equivalent of sky, thundering anew. *Do better in class. Better at games. Don't cheek the masters. Pay attention to your bed-making. Your hair. Your marks. The polish on your shoes. To matron. Your parents. Me.*

That same Friday, however, quite by chance and wholly out of sequence for once – just after Paul had observed Pheko and Spier, in fact – he was to be found darkening the main corridor as well, where the hapless Paul, who'd come inside, experienced his louring approach much as you might the onset of a rogue thundercloud.

'Ah,' he barked, 'Harvey! Aren't you forgetting something?'

'Sir?' said Paul, coming to a halt; to attention too, since it was unthinkable not to stand absolutely straight, with your hands at your sides, before Mr Wilson, who always stood that way himself.

'In a room not far from here,' elaborated the headmaster, 'you'll find Mrs MacWilliam. Mrs Stanford too, I think, this evening. Who've asked a favour of you, if I'm not mistaken. Come on, Harvey! High time you gave them your answer, isn't it? Don't run, though! You know the rule.'

'Thank you, sir,' said Paul, taking care to move at a suitable pace as he set off in the required direction. 'It's very thoughtful of you to remind me.'

'Glad to have my uses,' replied the headmaster – a comment which, with someone like Spier, would have been accompanied by a smile. Not with Mr Wilson, however. Thunderclouds don't show amusement.

Six

Whereas Mrs MacWilliam was *all* smile as she looked up from her desk. 'Well, well!' she said, nudging Mrs Stanford, who happened to be sitting alongside her. 'We've been on tenterhooks. Haven't we, Cynthia?'

'You could say that,' allowed Mrs Stanford, eyes also fixed on Paul from behind a pair of particularly pointy spectacles.

'And so?' queried Mrs MacWilliam. 'Don't keep us waiting. Do we or don't we have ourselves a monitor?' Going on to exclaim, when Paul nodded, 'What did I tell you, Cynthia! I knew we could rely on him.' She indicated the nearby trolley, piled high with books. 'Not quite supper yet – you could always start with those if you wanted.'

As Paul set about his task, the sense the library always gave him, of being a refuge, somewhere safe and secure, enfolded him again, and the rest of the week – Horton's having it in for him because of being leapfrogged over in the club hierarchy; not managing to hear what Lombard had wanted to tell him in the pool; getting a really bad mark for his history homework ('the causes of the Great Trek'); not doing brilliantly either in maths *or* geography, all of which his mother would question him about on Sunday; being accosted by the headmaster; and Spier, of course – Spier more than anything – this all began to recede and settle. It didn't go away exactly; but for a short while his concerns, his fears, his worries did abate.

'You're an absolute angel!' cried Mrs MacWilliam when, finally, he was done. 'Can't think how we were managing without you. Hey, Cynthia?'

'But now you'd better go wash those hands of yours,' was all that the less-effusive Mrs Stanford had to say. 'Look at the dust on them! Maybe that's another task, for another day. Don't you agree, Susan? The books clearly need it.'

Then the bell rang and, having promised to come back next week to dust, Paul hurried for the supper queue. In it, he found himself behind Slug, who, on registering Paul's arrival, turned to whisper, 'Your report and any stuff that goes with it needs to be written out, hey, before lights-out. That's what he says. I'll collect it after prep. Okay? Got that?'

The queue began shuffling forward – Stanford had meanwhile appeared at the top of the steps – though not before Slug had added, in a more conciliatory tone, 'I know it's difficult. I find it difficult too. Everyone does.'

Difficult! Talk about an understatement.

Still, needs must, and so, during the latter half of prep, having finished his history essay and oblivious, for once, to the sweet sounds emanating from the maids, Paul wrote up what he'd seen after swimming. Taking care, of course, to cover his writing with his left hand lest Stanford, who was still on duty, see what he was up to in the course of his frequent forays up and down the hall.

As Paul wrote, he began to fear that what he had to say was altogether too inconsequential. It amounted to so little, really, the distant scene he'd witnessed, even after he'd recorded every detail, making him wish – how he wished! – that he could have stolen Spier's anti-library. Next time he'd just have to try harder. There was no other way.

Then Stanford dismissed them and Slug leaned forward – he'd been sitting opposite – so that Paul could hand over his report, having first put it in an envelope, which he'd had the foresight to bring with him into prep and which he took particular care to seal.

'I knew you'd do it,' said Slug, pocketing the envelope. 'Otherwise why would the masters always say how reliable you are? Don't think I haven't noticed.'

Words which were still echoing, ironically, in Paul's head long after lights-out. What did it mean exactly, to be reliable? *Was* it something to be proud of? Or was it only another thing to worry about?

He lay there motionless, staring not at his usual patch of night sky but at the blank canvas of the adjacent, lowered blind, on which – as on a cinema screen – Spier was undressing again for him: tie, shirt, watch, shoes, socks, trousers, tight, white underpants. Then a cut and Spier was poised on the higher of the two diving boards, ready for his dive. A sunstruck, living statue; a latter-day Greek god, with Miss de Villiers pointing out his attributes, one by one.

Seven

IN MOKIMOLLE, my hosts for the evening are still keeping me company, even though I've finished my *bobotie* and am coming to the end of my dessert, a home-made *melk tert*, quite delicious, the provenance of which Lawrence has twice explained, first when I decided to order the dish; secondly, as the silent black waiter set it before me.

Throughout the meal, in fact, and despite his partner's desire to avoid '*blerrie* history', the man has clearly wanted – and managed – to talk of little else. He has that need, common to many white South Africans, to explain everything in terms of its genesis. As if he can thereby give his world greater coherence; contain it within a *laager* of words; make it less frightening.

And there is much, maintains Lawrence, to be frightened of. Urban violence: Johannesburg again, or Jozie, as he terms it. Rural violence – largely unreported, he says: vicious attacks on farmers and the like. (I think of those three staring men in the dusty Ford.) While the government, he adds, do nothing, *blerrie* monkeys. *Yissus!* Mismanagement and corruption on a scale you wouldn't believe. An African scale. Power shortages, presidential profligacy, the uncertain rand. Where to stop?

'Now, please, *skattie*,' pleads Giles. 'Since you ask.'

But he is just hitting his stride, is Lawrence. Though he does concede, maybe in deference to Giles' feelings, maybe in order to stop me, as a supposed European, feeling smug, that corruption is not exclusive to South Africa.

'Your pommie politicians too,' he says, 'can also be *skelms*, hey!'

'You know what a *skelm* is?' asks Giles.

I almost give myself away by nodding; but, in time, manage to ask artlessly, 'A... what... scoundrel?'

'Exactly,' says Lawrence. 'Politicians, hey! Say one thing, do another, think another. Except Mandela. I'll give you that. Though even he, hey, had his flaws. That poor first wife of his.'

His saying this about politicians makes me feel worse than I have already been feeling about my own twofold duplicity: not revealing either my origins, or that I share something else with them too, just as defining. I've come all this way after all these years and still I'm vulnerable to outside pressure. What would Spier have said? Or my parents, come to that. Slug. All three of the du Toits.

Their and other such faces (Mr Wilson's, Mrs MacWilliam's, Mosa's) hang in the gallery of my mind, a spectral echo of the family photos lining the walls of the du Toit residence. They watch. They take note. They continue to pass judgement.

'Tell me,' I say, endeavouring to change the course of the conversation, 'if I do want to scout around tomorrow, like you suggest, apart from the...' I almost say *koppie* '...the hill where you get the views – is there anything else I should be looking out for?'

It transpires that yes, there actually is: a modest museum of local history; a quite nice tea room; and, in Malan Street, a cottage where Herman Charles Bosman once stayed.

'You probably won't have heard of him,' says Giles, 'but he's one of our better-known writers. Or was. Dead now. It's not open, the cottage, Elsie Le Grange lives there these days. But still worth a look from the outside.'

'Nothing else?' I ask innocently.

Frowning, Giles plucks at his billowy shirt. 'Well,' he says, 'not really. I mean, there are a few shops, but nothing in them that you can't find somewhere else, and better.'

'A church?'

'*Ja*, a couple. Dutch Reformed, Anglican, a Methodist chapel.'

'Cemetery?'

There! I've asked it.

'Of course,' says Giles, in the dismissive tone of someone who takes it for granted that their cemetery can't possibly be of interest to visitors. 'It's on the outskirts. You pass it on the way to the *koppie*. *Ag*, and

I'm forgetting, silly me, the *vlei*. Sorry, I mean dam. Lake. That's there too, if you like birds.'

'Thank you,' I say, having learned all that I need. 'And now, if you'll excuse me ... ' I push back my chair. 'All that driving, it's quite tired me out. Delicious food, Lawrence. Thanks also, both of you, for your excellent company. You've been most informative. I do appreciate it.'

Am I trying too hard, I wonder, to sound like a pukka Englishman?

'Don't mention it,' says Lawrence, the sharpness of his face softening suddenly into a smile. 'My pleasure. Our pleasure. We enjoy people. It's why, hey, we started this in the first place, our little B&B. Isn't it, *skattie*?'

But Giles has floated to the door leading into the kitchen and is calling through it, 'Petrus! *Die borde!*' His ample frame, as he summons the silent waiter to clear away the plates, puts me in mind of Slug. He, too, could fill a doorway.

'See you in the morning,' I say, slipping away.

'*Slaap lekker,*' replies Lawrence.

Paul woke that Saturday feeling a good deal calmer than he had when falling asleep on the Friday. The thought, perhaps, of seeing his parents at cricket, having not been able to spend any significant time with them the previous Sunday. Or was it just that he'd survived another week? Whatever the reason, the unfurled blind no longer doubled as a cinema screen; it was simply an unfurled blind, quite blank. As was the sky – blue and cloudless.

Only Bentley major, in his role as dormitory monitor, could be deemed vexsome as he ordered them to strip their beds and put their dirty laundry in a pile by the door before fetching clean from Matron.

'Last one to finish,' he instructed, 'is a *vrot* tomato.'

Paul made it out of the dormitory first and had more or less completed his bed by the time Slug eventually came waddling back with his own clean sheets and pillow case to be met by a chorus of: '*Vrot* tomato! *Vrot* tomato!'

Not that Paul noticed particularly; he felt too calm still, and it wasn't until cricket that he became susceptible again to changes in the emotional atmosphere. Emerging from the main building to find his parents already on the sidelines, he immediately began running towards them, barely registering, for once, the unsuitable suit, or that Peggy was wearing a more than usually drab dress. A sort of sack. The very reverse of last weekend's frock.

'Hello, darling,' she said. Then the customary kiss, the customary questions. 'Must you always run? How were this morning's lessons?'

In essence, all just as it should be, excepting something untoward in Peggy's voice: a certain tightness, as if she was holding herself back – the first sign that maybe the afternoon wouldn't be easy.

'Hello, old fruit,' murmured Douglas. 'Pleased to see us?'

'Why wouldn't he be?'

'Just asking, that's all.'

'Your father!' sighed Peggy, with a sharp shake of her elegant head.

'What about me?'

Paul's parents didn't often argue – or not, anyway, that he was aware of – unless perhaps over trivialities, like Douglas mislaying the car keys, or Peggy taking too long in a shop; and even then it was bickering, really, rather than arguing.

But this sounded serious.

Paul looked from one to the other, then glanced about to see if anyone might have overheard. Thankfully, no one was near. Only – except he was closer to the pavilion than he was to them – Mr du Toit in conversation with an uncomfortable-looking Spier.

Quickly, Paul averted his gaze. The last thing he wanted, after yesterday, was to be caught staring at Spier.

Meanwhile, another master, old MacWilliam, homely like his wife but without her sweetness of nature, happened to lope by and say to Peggy, 'Has he confessed yet that he could have done better in this week's test?'

'Is that so, darling?' queried Peggy once the unhelpful master had moved on.

'Honestly!' said Douglas. 'Cut the lad some slack, why don't you?'

'You think his marks aren't important? After all the trouble we've been to, getting him in here?'

'It's the weekend, for Christ's sake, and I for one would like to watch the match, if that's all right with you? Having missed last week's.'

In usual adult fashion, they were behaving as though Paul weren't there.

'I thought we'd agreed,' said Peggy ominously, 'to keep off the subject of last weekend. And no swearing, please. *Pas devant.*'

'I agreed no such thing.'

'Really? Well, if only you could be this forceful when it comes to other matters, that's all I can say.'

'Meaning?'

'Oh, never mind. And anyway, last weekend, I was only trying to be polite.'

'Polite! So, simpering like that is just politeness, is it?'

'I beg your pardon?'

'You heard!'

'*Simpering*?'

'I could think of a few other choice phrases too.'

Thrusting an agitated hand into the pocket of her sack-like dress, Peggy yanked from it a lacy scrap of handkerchief, into which – fiercely – she blew her nose.

'If you knew how unfair you're being!' she said. 'We both ultimately want the same thing!'

'Not if it entails behaving like that, we don't.'

'For the umpteenth time, Douglas, my behaviour last weekend was not anything you need to worry about. I was simply trying—'

But here they were interrupted by Mr du Toit, who chose that precise moment to stride up and say, 'Peggy! Douglas! How are you both?'

And even if he hadn't, which he definitely did – I can still see his too-tight shorts and shirt, the cigarette that protruded from one corner of his mouth – I should certainly be curtailing the argument myself, since (hindsight again) I may be over-egging the pudding.

'I really, really enjoyed last Sunday,' Mr du Toit went on. 'And not only me, hey. Usually Violet gets to cook for just the three of us, not exactly a challenge, so *she* says especially, come again, please! Will you?'

Douglas made no reply, leaving Peggy to say, again with that tightness in her voice, no hint of a simper, 'We enjoyed it too.'

'So okay, then!' grinned Mr du Toit, extinguishing his cigarette underfoot, 'how about the exeat after tomorrow? You can check out the farm a bit and, like I say, Violet will be over the moon. All her Christmases in one.'

'Well,' said Douglas, 'that's very kind. Very generous. But next weekend, as it happens, we're busy. Aren't we, Peggy?'

'*Ag*, that's too bad!' said Mr du Toit, appearing not to notice the look of total surprise Peggy was shooting in Douglas's direction. 'So we must just make another date, then. Maybe the week after? And for next week, can we at least have Paul? *He* can come out again with Andre. Can't he?'

Paul was fully expecting – hoping, even – that Douglas would again step in. But this time Peggy got there ahead of him.

'He most certainly can,' she said firmly. 'You'd like that, darling, wouldn't you? Another exeat with your friend? How sweet, Koos. Thank you.' She turned her gaze on Douglas, daring him to contradict her.

'That's settled, then,' said Mr du Toit with a broad smile. 'Fantastic!' And, stepping close to Peggy – which made Douglas almost flinch, Paul noticed – he added quietly, 'It isn't easy for him, not having both parents around at the same time. He gets lonely. Like his pa.'

Peggy's cheeks coloured again, just as they had at the farm, and her hand went to her throat. Simultaneously, Douglas's flinch became a deep frown and, for a moment, time seemed almost to stand still. All that could be heard was the sound of a bat connecting with the ball and the umpire (Stanford) shouting, 'Six!' Then Mr du Toit stepped back and looked sideways. Green eyes narrowing, his smile becoming narrower too, more of a snarl really than a smile, he called out, 'About the Congress of Democrats, don't let me forget, there's an article you really ought to read. I'll bring it with next time.'

'You do that,' said a curt voice: Spier's.

'Over!'

Out on the field, the players were changing position.

On Sundays, breakfast was routinely followed by an inspection, during which that term's monitor would slowly pace the length of the dormitory, making sure the sheets on every bed had been properly changed the morning before, that counterpanes were smooth, and corners neatly tucked in, hospital-style. Lockers would also be inspected, with curtains being lifted so that the contents could be scanned for any prohibited items or hint of slovenliness. Then, and only then, was the dormitory dismissed, leaving you free at last (providing you didn't need to stay behind to remake your bed or rearrange your locker) to grab your satchel and dash outside, for no master – except the head – would try to stop running in the corridor on the morning of an exeat. Not even Stanford.

That Sunday, however, Paul didn't dash, but dawdled rather. After the way in which his parents had argued at cricket, he was actually not eager to start the day, with the result that Matron, coming ghost-like upon him in the corridor – it was her white uniform, white shoes and white cap that gave her the appearance of a ghost – was induced to comment, 'Problems with your bed, Harvey? That's not like you.'

'No, Matron, my bed was fine.'

'Or do more chores await you at home, perhaps?' She smiled: her starched carapace was only part of the picture; there was also a kindly face to consider. 'Dragging your feet won't make them go away, you know.'

With this, she turned into another dormitory, thus allowing him to continue alone down the stairs to where, from inside the hall, he was briefly lulled by the music of the maids before emerging at last through the front door, where he encountered smelly old Botma at the top of the steps, keeping an eye on everyone's departure.

The master pointed with a flourish of his smoky pipe to where the Cortina was parked. 'Have a good exeat, Harvey,' he grunted.

'Yes, sir,' replied Paul, starting down the steps. 'Thank you, sir. You as well, sir.'

Also parked in the drive was the du Toit truck, which Paul had therefore to pass as he approached the

Cortina. In the driver's seat was Mr du Toit; next to him, the disdainful Laura; behind them, her brother. Then he noticed that in Mr du Toit's meaty hand was a familiar-looking sheet of paper, pale against his suntan – the very sheet, no less, on which was written Paul's account of what he'd seen on Friday after swimming.

As it had in the changing room that afternoon, his stomach went into instant freefall and it was a somewhat stunned young boy who climbed into the Cortina.

'You took your time,' said Douglas. 'We're almost the last. Well, us and ... ' He didn't finish the sentence, however. Instead, looking searchingly at Paul, he asked, 'Anything wrong?'

Paul looked away. 'No, Dad. Why?'

'You sure?' Douglas turned the key. 'Because we both thought you seemed a bit subdued yesterday. At the match, I mean.' He engaged the clutch. 'Were you?' The car pulled into the drive, overtaking the dusty truck.

'I'm fine, Dad, really,' said Paul. 'Don't fuss. You and Mum always make such a fuss.'

Face still turned aside, he was staring at the passing houses. The high hedges and elaborate gates; the glimpses of garden boys at work on immaculate lawns; the sprinklers that threw glittering arcs, seemingly of diamonds, into the morning air; the open garages; the spick cars. Affluence; security; the status quo. What St Luke's was grooming him for.

Apropos nothing, or so it seemed, Douglas said, 'Well, adults can be fallible. Remember that and you won't go far wrong in life. Oh, and while I think of it, the windscreen needs cleaning. All these poor squashed insects. I can hardly see out. Could you, old fruit? At some stage today. Please?'

Matron had been right: chores did await.

Nor was that the only chore in prospect, since after they arrived home and Paul had said hello to Peggy and Mosa in the kitchen and answered his mother's added questions – what had the week's meals been like? Had he finished his tuck? Bowel movements? Fingernails? – she at once took him to task about his test results. Why had Mr MacWilliam felt a need to comment? What exactly had his mark been? She then demanded to know if he had any exercise books in his satchel, which lay where he'd dropped it earlier, on the kitchen counter. In it he found quite a few: science, maths and, by chance, geography, containing the test in question. He also happened to have his geography textbook with him, the one from which the test had been set.

'Excellent!' cried Peggy. 'So this morning, dear, I want you to go to your room and look again at that chapter.'

'But, Mum, it's Sunday! I never...'

Argument was useless, however. Not only had Peggy made up her mind, she'd done so with the same tightness in her voice that he'd noticed yesterday.

To do, perhaps, with the dispute he'd overheard at cricket? Or was it the fact that, as she now let slip, Father Ashley was unexpectedly coming to lunch again.

'Poor man, when he phoned last night, well, I don't think I've ever heard such distress...'

'Why? What's happened?'

'All in good time. Geography first. Mosa, will you pour Paul a glass of milk? Oh, and you can help yourself to a biscuit, dear, if you like. But just the one! We don't want you spoiling your appetite.'

Then out she went, through the scullery, to deal with her hopeless garden.

'Young master will soon do his work,' said Mosa with a comforting smile. 'You will see.'

She had, in her hand, Paul's satchel, wanting no doubt to get at his tuck tin and clear it of crumbs before Peggy refilled it. But in so doing, she revealed something else besides: Pheko's blood-stained handkerchief.

'*Hayi Khona*!' she gasped. 'Did the young master hurt himself? And this is not the right handkerchief! From where does it come, this handkerchief?'

'Oh, I just borrowed it from a friend,' said Paul with attempted nonchalance. 'In my class. You don't know him.'

'Then Mosa won't ask,' said the maid. 'But she will make it clean again. For this friend in your class.'

Which had, in fact, been Paul's secret hope: to get the handkerchief laundered at home. He knew that, if he put it in with his school washing, even trickier questions might be asked.

Meanwhile, having tucked the handkerchief into the pocket of her apron, Mosa was crossing to the fridge.

'Can the master carry the glass himself?' she asked, fetching out a milk bottle. 'Or must Mosa bring it for him?'

'No, thanks, I'll be fine. Really.'

'Then Mosa will finish the potatoes and Madam will call when the food it is ready.'

Alone in his room at last, Paul set down his milk and biscuit on his desk, removed his school books from his satchel, then fell into his chair.

Before him lay an airmail letter, addressed in a well-known and much-loved hand. Tearing it open, he read:

Dear Paul,

Will you be sitting at your desk as you read this? I'm writing it at mine, looking out at the garden, long past its best. Soon the gardener and I will have to start preparing the beds for winter. While you of course get hotter and hotter! Isn't that a funny thought?

How is school? Are you still feeling lonely? Your mother wrote last week that you've made a new friend. I'm so glad. Friends are important. You don't ever have many of them in life, not real friends, but those that you do can last the whole of it. I've been very lucky with mine and I hope you will be too.

When I finish this, I must take the bus into town. Can you believe, I've allowed my library books to go overdue! Silly me. Now I'll get a fine. Two Jean Plaidys and a Winston Graham. He's very good. One day you must read him, instead of all those comics. You're not such a little boy any longer.

I also have to pop into the chemist's for my prescription, then the bakery for a loaf of bread. One of their cobs, I think, if they have one. When your grandfather was still alive, that's what he would always buy, if I sent him. Mouth-watering, he always said.

I've been talking to your mother about visiting.
Don't tell her I've told you, because nothing is certain
yet, but she says I should come this winter and I'm
starting to think that might not be such a bad idea.
Some of your heat in exchange for our cold! When
you get older you really feel the cold and I've not been
well of late. Feeble old thing that I am!
Anyway, a big hug from –
your loving Grandmama

After her name, she'd made a neat line of crosses, each
one a kiss. Paul did the same when writing to her. Slowly,
lingeringly he traced them with his finger, then put the letter
down and, because he could no longer help himself, let the
hot tears gush down his cheeks. Until eventually, aware that
if he didn't open his geography book further misery would
ensue, he rubbed at his eyes with the back of his hand and,
happening to look upwards at the same time, fixed on the
second verse of the poem that hung above his desk:

If you can bear to hear the truth you've spoken
Twisted by knaves to make a trap for fools,
Or watch the things you gave your life to, broken,
And stoop and build 'em up with worn-out tools...

If, if, if!

It's surprising to me, which writings from childhood I do
and don't remember. My grandmother's letter, now: of
course I would remember that. I remember pretty much

all her letters, even have most of them with me still. My old diary as well: that has similarly survived. Though not the key. The key is lost.

Wouldn't Freud have a field day!

But Kipling? Why can I, to this day, recite all four of that poem's stanzas as confidently as I can the club rules? Another field day? Although, at the time, young Paul simply took for granted what he did and didn't keep in mind. And anyway, that Sunday he had other things to concentrate upon – like, for example, the unexpected reappearance of Father Ashley at lunch.

'So!' began Douglas once they'd been served and Mosa had withdrawn. 'They just turned up yesterday, without warning, and that was that?'

'Well,' replied the priest, running an anxious hand through the spikes of his hair – he kept doing this as he talked, or else would tug at his ear, restless fingers forever on the prowl – 'to the extent that I'd already been worried about Simon's behaviour, we had due warning there, I suppose. But that they were planning to ban him ...!'

'No phone call, nothing?'

'Unless you count Sergeant Avenant. I think I've already told you – did I, Peggy, when I phoned? – that he called on Friday to say he wanted to ask me something about the church hall. Nothing important, he said, but would we be in on Saturday? Nice man, I've always liked Avenant. Do either of you know him? No, why should you! When do law-abiding citizens ever need to make the acquaintance of their local policemen? Though it could also be a coincidence, of course. Anyway, yesterday after lunch, they did – yes, indeed – just appear at the door. Two of them, in safari suits – security police, they said, or Special Branch, I forget which – asking for Simon, whom they then handed a set of papers, which he had to sign, and now he's banned, the idiot, and under house arrest. Simple as that.'

'Douglas, pass Father Ashley the gravy,' said Peggy. 'And you, Paul dear, what about you? It looks as if you could do with some too.'

'Like this Helen Joseph woman, then, from last weekend,' said Douglas, reaching as instructed for the gravy. 'Bloody hell!'

'Douglas!'

'Precisely!' said the priest. 'Every day, for the next five years – or is it once a week? I forget now, though it's in the papers they served – anyway, he has to report to police headquarters. *And* he must be home every evening by six and can't leave again until seven the next morning. At weekends, it's from six on the Friday all the way through to Monday morning, without a break. Plus there are already a couple of men parked outside, sitting in their car, keeping watch. *I'm* allowed to be in the room with him, but no one else. If we have visitors, Simon must make himself scarce.'

'And the maid?' asked Peggy. 'What about her?'

'That, they didn't say. A doctor's all right, though.'

'So who else knows?' asked Douglas. 'Did you mention it at church?'

'I did wonder whether to. Though to be honest I didn't know how to put it. So few people know Simon as you do. Or our situation generally. So no, so far you're the only ones.'

'Well, we won't say a word in that case,' said Peggy. 'Will we, Douglas? Not to anyone. Promise.'

'I don't suppose,' was Douglas's next question, 'anyone has said why? The men who came? Simon himself?'

'I fear Simon and I haven't exactly been communicating,' said the priest. 'I intend to, of course. In time, I intend to find out in every detail what he's been up to, stupid boy, instead of concentrating on his studies like a worthwhile student.'

'And the security police?'

Father Ashley shook his head. 'Not forthcoming either, I'm afraid. They would only talk to him. On Monday I shall have to call a lawyer. Luckily, there's a man the church sometimes uses, who should be able to advise.'

Peggy then wanted to know what Simon was doing for lunch. Father Ashley must take back some food with him, she insisted. There were lots of vegetables left over.

'Funny!' she added. 'We came here because of what this country offers; now this.'

'Not funny, then,' said Douglas.

'Or if Evelyn and I had stayed in Bedfordshire,' agreed Father Ashley, 'she might still be alive. No malaria in Bedfordshire, after all.'

'*And* things grow there,' added Peggy with a rueful laugh. 'Garden-wise, I mean. Willy-nilly, they just grow and grow. Not that I'm for one minute suggesting ... '

'But you can't look back,' said Douglas. 'That way madness lies.'

After lunch, the adults retired to the lounge for coffee, Paul to his room to rest, his mind spinning from a meal which, at moments, had been like General Knowledge with Spier, where they'd also discussed house arrest. Whether or not a home should, could be used as a jail, with Spier saying: *Can we ever become our own jailors? Can we be tricked into locking ourselves up and throwing away the key simply by not doing or saying things that we know other people might not want us to do or say?*

Spier, who was a friend of Simon's – and, with this thought, a light came on in Paul's head. He saw, or thought he saw, what might lie behind du Toit's tasks. Du Toit wanted him to watch Spier because Spier was like his friend, Simon. A potential danger to the state. Which was why du Toit was in turn telling his father what Paul had discovered, because his father sometimes did things, or so du Toit had intimated, for the government; so who better to know about Spier than Mr du Toit, in case something needed to be done to stop Spier before things went too far, just as Simon had been stopped. Especially if Spier was talking to Pheko. Because everyone knew from history – take Sharpeville – what happened when black people got hold of the wrong ideas.

Politics! It had to do with politics. With keeping South Africa safe.

Then one final, almost subliminal thought: how utterly convenient it would be for Paul should Mr du Toit succeed in reining Spier in. For, ever since their encounter at the pool, he'd been wanting – how he wanted! – the master to stop taking up so much space in his head.

Feeling a whole lot lighter suddenly, he knelt before his cupboard and took out his treasured diary. He wasn't sure he'd be able to write all of this down; he wasn't even sure he wanted to. But he must at least record being in du Toit's club – what that felt like. And the farm a little. Laura. Becoming a library monitor. It had been a momentous fortnight.

The diary fell open at one of its earliest entries.

Granny wants me to go and live in England, he read. *This is a dangerous country, she says. She worries that I'm not safe here.*

But now – how amazing – he could also write that, in his own small way, he was helping to make it safer.

What did the poem say? *And stoop and build 'em up with worn-out tools...*

Unscrewing his pen, he flipped through the creamy pages until he came to the correct date, then started to write, stopping only when he'd got to Sunday October 21st, where he recorded that Father Ashley came for lunch because his son, Simon, had been placed under house arrest. About Spier, he said nothing.

Relocking the diary, he briefly toyed with the idea of taking it into school with him, as du Toit had suggested. Then thought better of it. Once had been enough. So instead, having returned the diary to Teddy's safekeeping, he decided to pull out a *Classics Illustrated*. There was still time before tea, he reckoned, especially as, after doing his geography, he'd also dealt with the car windscreen before lunch.

A Tale of Two Cities, why not? Something to tell Granny in his next letter. That actually his comics were quite educational. So there! *And* he would tell her about the library. Becoming a monitor. She'd not dare tease him about that. That, she'd understand in a flash.

Father Ashley, with Evensong still to perform, had left by the time Paul emerged from his room, and it was just the three of them for tea, where the by now inconsequential talk was largely of the recently opened Civic Theatre in Johannesburg. Apparently, Peggy and Douglas had been to see something there called *A Man for All Seasons*.

'Starved as we are of culture,' said Peggy. 'Though I do wish we didn't always get palmed off with the West End understudy. And those acoustics! You'd think they could at least get that right these days. If the Romans could... In a purpose-built venue. Vulgar-looking, too, don't you agree, Douglas? No wonder there have been all those articles in the paper.'

'Absolutely, my dear, absolutely.'

Peggy glanced at her watch. 'But I'd better start filling your tin, Paul. Any special requests?'

Seven

'Funny old day,' said Douglas in the car later, 'one way and another. Funny weekend, really. And now, next weekend, we won't be seeing you at all, will we? Because, if I'm remembering right, there's no cricket for us to come to next weekend. Away matches only for the rest of term. Yes? A pity.'

'I don't have to go on Sunday if you don't want,' said Paul. 'Honestly, Dad, I don't mind if you tell Mr du Toit I can't. He'll probably be there still.'

But with a firm shake of his head Douglas replied quietly, 'I think we both know that isn't on the cards, don't we, old fruit? Now give your old dad a kiss.' This as, reluctantly, Paul was pushing open the car door after Douglas had drawn up in the school drive. 'Have you got everything? Did Mum pack enough tuck for a fortnight?'

But of course she had. More than enough. Just as Mosa had also thought to ensure his satchel carried within it an ironed and laundered handkerchief.

Eight

THAT TUESDAY, not through General Knowledge for once but a set of Chinese whispers initially, certain potentially catastrophic events unfolding on the other side of the globe began to make themselves felt at St Luke's.

A pale-faced matron awoke them. Usually, this was done cheerfully: she would joke about how lazy they all were, threaten those who didn't leap from their beds with a dose perhaps of castor oil. That Tuesday, however, not only was she pale-faced, she was tight-lipped too. No jokes of any description were forthcoming, not even feeble ones.

And at breakfast, Stanford, who was reading that day's paper while keeping an eye on them all from his vantage point on the stage, took particular care, if anyone approached, to fold his paper over, obscuring the headline.

Throughout the morning, too, whenever any teachers crossed paths and thought they were out of earshot, there was much whispering, all very urgent.

'Something's up,' said Horton in the queue for lunch. 'Otherwise why is everyone acting so strange?'

'I saw Stanford's paper at breakfast,' said Slug. 'There was something in it about a blockade.'

'And I heard old MacWilliam in the corridor,' volunteered Kintock, 'talking to Botma about Castrol.'

'The motorcar oil?'

'I suppose.'

'My father,' said Labuschagne, 'thinks Valvoline is better.'

Not that this was to the point, but, when Kintock spoke, Labuschagne always had to add something.

'Maybe there'll be an announcement at lunch,' said Bentley major hopefully.

'You think?'

'If something's happened that we ought to know about,' said Strover, 'sure.'

'But if everyone's whispering, then isn't that because they *don't* want us to know? Duh!'

And indeed, no announcement was made at lunch, other than what old MacWilliam had to say about that afternoon's games.

Only in the moments just before lights-out did they finally discover what was afoot. Spier was on duty that night and so, Spier being Spier, as he stood by the door with one hand on the switch, Lombard felt emboldened enough to ask, 'Sir, please, sir, before you turn the lights out, sir, can you tell us what's been happening? Why is everyone acting so strange?'

Lowering his hand, Spier looked appraisingly from bed to bed. Then he said, the words as clear as they were grave, 'This morning we heard that President Kennedy went on television last night to announce that Soviet missiles have been discovered in Cuba.'

An alert silence greeted this revelation, broken eventually by Eedes, who asked, 'Soviet, sir?'

'Russian, Eedes, Russian! You really ought to know these things.'

'Sorry, sir.'

'Of both the medium- and intermediate-range ballistic variety, it seems.' The words were still clear; still grave.

'Ballistic, sir?' ventured Strover. 'What's ballistic?'

'Rockets, basically, that have some nuclear capability.' Again Spier scanned the beds. 'And Cuba, of course, for those of you who don't know even this much, is an island in the Caribbean, very close to America, but with Soviet sympathies.'

'When you say nuclear, sir,' persisted Strover, 'do you mean like the atomic bomb? Like Hiroshima?'

'I'm afraid that's exactly what I mean,' said Spier. 'Fingers seem to be very much on the button. Sorry.'

An image came to Paul of two men, both in uniform, glaring at each other across a desk that featured, on its surface, a red button of cartoonish proportions. Then one of their fingers suddenly jabbed down on the button and the cartoon exploded into a fireball, a mushroom cloud; screaming people with skin peeling from their backs. Images from a film they'd been shown once about the Second World War. He glanced fearfully about him. The other boys seemed to be seeing things too, for no one spoke and it was left to Spier to conclude, 'But the headmaster will talk to you in more detail tomorrow. Meanwhile, just remember, hey – we're actually on the other side of the world. Not in the immediate firing line. Not even close.'

Then, as in Paul's cartoonish vision, his finger jabbed at the light switch and they were plunged into darkness.

Speculative whispering, a great deal of it, should have started up at this point; it usually did after earth-shattering announcements. But that night, strangely, there was pure silence, within which Paul lay staring dumbly at his personal oblong of starry sky. Was it his imagination, or had the stars come nearer somehow? As if they too wished to tell him something.

It was after breakfast the next morning that the headmaster delivered his promised address, with everyone at their tables still, emptied bowls of porridge in front of them and a few maids just beginning to gather near the door. Normally, when Mr Wilson made a speech from the stage like this, the boys would sit facing him on benches specially lined up for the occasion. This morning, however, they were left facing each other across their empty bowls and the headmaster's words were a sort of broadside, fired in contravention, as it were, of standard procedure – rather like the missiles he was telling them about.

Quoting from President Kennedy's speech, he said the Cuban missiles had been termed: *a reckless and provocative threat to world peace* by the Soviet Union which required: *a full retaliatory response*. Kennedy was asking Khrushchev, the communist leader, to *abandon his course of world domination* in order to *move the world back from the abyss of destruction*.

Then, lest all of this frighten them unduly, he went on to say that America had already instituted an arms quarantine against Cuba. Any ship bound for the island with a cargo of offensive weapons would be turned back by the American navy, who had the island surrounded. In addition, they were sending reinforcements to a base there called Guantanamo Bay. And, last but not least, they were calling for an emergency meeting of the Security Council of the United Nations, keeper of world peace.

The headmaster even smiled, not something the boys often saw him do, as he ended with, 'People talk about *die rooi gevaar*, to use a vulgar phrase. And with reason, obviously. We, however, can count ourselves lucky, I think, that we live where we do, in a country determined to hold communism at bay. Nothing horrible is going to happen at St Luke's. You have my word. So let us just get on with our lives, okay, like good South Africans. Without fear, without hesitation. Trusting to God.'

Which was, of course, asking the impossible, and the speculation that had failed to start after lights-out the night before began in earnest after breakfast, leaping from group to group like a veld fire until, by evening, the entire school was ablaze. Even in class, be it science with Botma, maths with Stanford (Stanford's class too), art with Miss de Villiers, or geography with old MacWilliam, rumour spread virtually unchecked, and the headmaster's exhortation for them to get on with their lives like good South Africans lay smouldering in its wake, quite burned out.

Those who knew about aviation talked knowledgeably of a plane called the U-2, since that was how the missiles had first been spotted, apparently. While those who knew about missiles spelled out in ever greater detail the differences between medium- and intermediate-range. Others debated the weather. What would it take, wind-wise, they wondered, for any fallout to be carried to South Africa? How many days after a bomb dropped before their world changed forever? Stories were swapped about both Hiroshima and Nagasaki, using more images from that film they'd seen. Not so much the buildings that splintered – they knew they weren't close enough for that. But people's skin peeling off. Or people just walking along one minute, falling down dead the next, *sommer so*. Because that was how lethal fallout could be: lethal *and* invisible, like a virus. *Black rain*, as it was also called, according to Strover, who'd heard his father use the expression once. The world's ultimate nightmare.

Another question, perhaps the most crucial of all, was: how would they actually know if a bomb had been dropped? How exactly would the start of a nuclear holocaust be signalled?

Lombard had the answer.

'We'll see it in the sunset,' he proclaimed. 'If there's a nuclear explosion on the other side of the world, what happens in the atmosphere there will be reflected in ours.'

They were standing in a group of four in the playground: Lombard, Horton, Slug and Paul.

'How?' asked Horton.

'The sunset'll be redder. More intense. If you like, more beautiful.'

'That's weird,' murmured Slug, almost into Paul's ear, he was that close. 'Just as the world's coming to an end.'

'So I vote we all keep watch,' continued Lombard, warming to his thesis. 'In groups is best and someone should also keep a log.'

'Harvey's good at that,' said Slug, still close. 'Aren't you, Harvey?'

'*Ag*, I can do a log,' said Horton. 'There's plenty space in my old geography book.'

'So let's start tonight,' said Lombard. 'And I'll also ask Eedes, he'll be good, to organise some other groups, then we can take it in turns.'

'What about Eedes?' The question was put by du Toit, who'd appeared alongside them. 'What's Eedes organising?'

There was a moment's silence, during which Paul experienced a miniature revelation. Just as the stars had seemed subtly altered the night before, in the wake of Spier's first giving them the news, so he now saw du Toit differently as well. The stars had appeared nearer; du Toit, by contrast, loomed less large suddenly, despite the fierceness with which he was asking, 'So are you going to tell me, Lombard, or do I have to force it out of you?' More urgent matters had diminished him.

'You and whose army?'

'We're forming a group,' said Slug nervously, 'to watch the sunset, that's all.'

'Why?'

'Because if there's a nuclear explosion on the other side of the world,' Slug continued, parrot-fashion, like when reading the club rules, 'what happens up in the atmosphere will be reflected in our sunset here. Isn't that right, Lombard?'

'I see,' said du Toit, cool eyes assessing each of them in turn. 'Okay, so in that case I reckon I'll join you.'

But Lombard wasn't having it.

'Form your own group, du Toit,' he said. 'You're not welcome in mine. Got that?'

Under normal circumstances, du Toit would have lashed out at this point, and a scuffle might have ensued. There were, after all, three club members on hand to lend support. But, amazingly, he did no such thing. Instead, he just stared hard at Lombard before eventually turning to Slug and saying, 'So, are you coming, or aren't you?'

Furthermore, he didn't try to encourage Paul or Horton to leave as well, a fact which Lombard noted gloatingly as he watched du Toit and Slug move off. 'That'll teach him,' he said. 'And at least he didn't pick on you too, hey, even though you're also under his command. You know something: I'm really glad he chucked me out. What sort of friend *is* it, hey, who always has to be on top?'

Now was the moment, Paul thought, to ask what Lombard had been meaning to tell him in the pool; but with Horton present he didn't quite dare – and anyway, Horton had already returned them to the subject of the sunset.

'If we meet between supper and prep,' he was saying, freckled face aflame, 'we can start tonight. Carp the deus. Am I saying it right?'

Word of Lombard's plan had spread as fast during supper as all the day's other rumours, with the consequence that maybe half the school, broken up into small groups, gathered in the playground before prep to scan the sky for each nuance of that day's sunset: the position and shape of any clouds, the speed with which those clouds changed colour, the colour not only of the clouds but of the sky itself, every gradation of it as the heavens underwent their twilight transformation: red to orange to pink to purple to black.

Of course, there was, on this first evening, nothing as yet with which to compare any observations; but careful notes were nonetheless made so that, tomorrow, the fearful business of assessing whether or not their days might be numbered could properly begin.

Paul stood with Lombard and Horton and Bentley major, who'd also joined them. No Slug – doubtless he was in the clutches of du Toit still, except not to watch the sunset apparently, since the pair of them weren't anywhere in evidence. Only as everyone was vanishing into prep did he appear – du Toit too, in the distance – to inform Paul, having waddled up to him, that on Friday there was to be another club meeting, immediately after games. Got that?

'Where have you two been?'

But Slug had a more pressing question of his own. 'How did it go? Scope anything?'

'You should have joined us, if you're so keen.'

'I would if I could've, like a shot. But it isn't always my choice. You know that.'

'Choice!' exclaimed Spier at the start of next day's General Knowledge Club. 'Today I want us to consider the question of choice. How we make choices and what happens sometimes if we don't when maybe we need to. Or if people don't like our choices, once made. Ourselves included.'

An uncertain murmur greeted this prolix introduction. For what they were burning to talk about rather was, of course, missiles.

'You're not interested in my choice of subject?' asked Spier, giving the word an ironic emphasis.

'Well, sir,' said Bentley major. 'If you don't mind, sir, we do actually have quite a lot of questions about what's been happening in Cuba and is there going to be a bomb, sir?'

'Again, a matter of choice,' said Spier, re-emphasising the word. 'But okay, I guess we should put all of this into some sort of context.'

Then, as I remember, he explained in detail about Cuba and Batista and how America felt about Cuba's new ruler, Castro. 'The United States regards communism pretty much as our own leaders do. *Die rooi gevaar*, to borrow your favourite phrase, du Toit. And now a favourite of our esteemed headmaster's as well, it would appear.' Then came a bit about the Bay of Pigs and how that failed American invasion had worsened an already tense situation. 'The rest you know from the headmaster,' he concluded, coming to rest like always against his untidy desk. 'Pretty much. But the background is important. It affects, or should, how we view what is happening today. So, with this in mind, I'd like us, please, to try to look at the situation in terms of the choices that have been made. Is it inevitable, what's happened, or could it have been avoided? Do we accept what President Kennedy says at face value? Or do we also want to know the Russian point of view? And, at the risk of navel-gazing, do we let what's happening outside our borders make us forget what's happening at home?'

Here, I'm fairly sure, he made reference to a black man wearing a jackal-skin *kaross* in a nearby court. Oh, and I also remember that he had rings under his eyes and had cut himself shaving. There was a small plaster on his cheek.

'I have a friend,' he said next, or words to this effect, 'a sometime friend, who's paying dearly – like Helen Joseph, with actual house arrest – for what he believes in. Should he have made that choice? Or should he have kept his mouth shut? Because I'm sure that's all he did: shoot his mouth off. And what would I have done, in his place? Instead of hiding away in a posh boys' school, teaching a partisan version of this country's history. What sort of choice is that?

'And you? What are *your* choices, boys? As our country's future?'

Which is upon us finally, in all its complexity, from silly things like my spurious fear of dusty Fords to overdecorated B&Bs to the negligible distance still remaining on this particular section of my journey. Not that coming to the end of it will necessarily provide, in modern parlance, closure. Any more than our second sunset watch provided certainty.

As before, the group scanned the horizon intently, asking:

Were there any changes from yesterday?

(None they could discern.)

Except weren't the shades of pink in the sky maybe pinker?

(Just fractionally perhaps.)

Tending towards red?

As Horton made a note, Lombard said, 'Wasn't that weird this afternoon? With Spier? And what's with du Toit, hey, and *die rooi gevaar*? Doesn't everyone say that?'

Paul wondered if he should explain about the note du Toit had once tried to pass him. However, since this would have been to put into words how cruelly du Toit used to treat him, he chose instead – here was a choice! – to remain silent. It wasn't as if Lombard and Horton didn't already know about his treatment at du Toit's hands – almost everyone in the school, even juniors, must have known about the theft of his diary – but still, no need to spell it out.

'Spier doesn't like du Toit,' said Horton. 'He's always looking at him *skeef*. It should be Slug, actually, in General Knowledge. I know he's a bit of a drip, but Spier doesn't mind Slug so much and Slug's not stupid. It just looks like he is.'

'Something else that should happen,' mused Lombard, 'is that you should *sommer* leave du Toit's club.'

'Me?' said Horton.

'*Ja*, of course. After what happened last time, like you were telling me.' He turned to Paul. 'This isn't against you, Harvey, you don't make the rules, but du Toit shouldn't change them just because he feels like it. The tasks are never secret. That's half the fun. So why yours?'

For one chilling moment, Paul feared he would have to explain what du Toit had asked him to do. But in the event Horton interposed with, '*Ja*, maybe you're right. I mean, who cares about his stinky club anyway! Now that the world's about to end.'

'So what exactly happened?' asked Paul, finding the courage at last, 'that made him expel you, Lombard?'

'I was going to tell you the other day,' said Lombard. 'But then you dive-bombed us,' he added, addressing Horton.

'Sorry,' said the dive-bomber. 'I was still quite *voes* at becoming number four.'

'So anyway,' Lombard went on, 'it was his sister actually, when I got invited to the farm once, who gave me the idea. All I told him was not to get so angry. With his mother and stuff. My parents are getting divorced too and so okay, it isn't my mother who's leaving, it's my dad, he's moving in with his secretary, and sure, it isn't nice – but same diffs. It's not like it's du Toit's fault his mother ran away. And he does still get to see her. Hell, I'd be glad if my mother wasn't always around to boss me about. He should count his lucky stars.'

'So you just told him,' said Paul, making sure he'd understood, 'not to get angry with his mother because she's left his father? And he expelled you?'

Lombard nodded, glasses flashing with the last of the light. 'I was only trying to help. Because of how unhappy he can get. But I suppose I got too close.'

'And now it's Slug!' snorted Horton, 'who's close. *Yissus!*' He closed his notebook and returned his fountain pen to his pocket; the evening's watch had ended.

'I'll check with the other groups after prep,' said Bentley major, who'd been largely silent up to now, as the four of them turned towards the classrooms. 'See if anyone's maybe noticed something we didn't. But so far, so good, hey! No bomb yet. Maybe the world won't blow up after all.'

In the distance, not far from the school's perimeter, stood one other group whose watch still hadn't ended, or so it looked. The group comprised du Toit, Slug, Labuschagne, Kintock and Strover. The rest of du Toit's club, in other words, excepting only Paul and Horton.

Going on appearances, Slug was the group's record-keeper; at any rate, he had in his pudgy hands the clipboard he used for club meetings. So maybe they hadn't only been watching the sunset? Maybe du Toit had called an impromptu club meeting ahead of the scheduled one, without using the club house for once *or* informing the other two members, who had shown such awful disobedience by daring to be part of Lombard's sunset watch.

For a split second, Paul was tempted to run over and ask. But then the bell rang and the group dispersed, revealing as they did so that, parked outside in the street, near to where they'd been standing, was an occupied car. He could tell it was occupied because, in its interior, there were the glowing tips of two cigarettes, one where the driver would be sitting, one for a passenger. Although he didn't, in fact, give either the car or its smoking occupants much thought as he went with the others towards their classroom and that evening's homework: an essay (fifty words minimum) on the establishment of the first Boer Republic.

The club meeting would inevitably be where, Paul imagined as he made his solitary way there the next day, he and Horton would face any chastisement. Was further expulsion on the cards, perhaps, because of their joint disrespect? Or a severe dressing-down? An especially difficult task? To his surprise, he then discovered that he didn't greatly care. It might even mean he didn't have to go with du Toit on Sunday – a blessing.

Truly, something fundamental had shifted in the course of the week; the world was no longer quite what it had been. A development for which, even though it came at a potentially fatal price, he was ultimately quite grateful.

He descended into the ditch to find – another surprise – that he was in advance of the others. The club house appeared empty; only a couple of the smaller huts, further off, showed signs of occupancy. Faint scuffling came from one, a snatch of high-pitched giggling from another. He took a few steps forward, whereupon – cicada-like – the giggling stopped. Those juniors certainly knew to be wary in the presence of a senior! Even if by all accounts this still hadn't stopped them from daring to venture inside du Toit's hut when no one was there. Did they not realise that they might, as a consequence, face attack? He could warn them, of course; but why on earth would he do that? Seniors never involved themselves in junior affairs. Not unless they had a screw loose.

Returning thoughtfully to du Toit's hut, he stood for a moment by the door, half listening to the giggles start up again. Then – again a surprise; he hadn't known he wanted to do this – he took hold of the wonky doorknob and stepped inside.

No huddled forms now; no Slug with his clipboard; no captain seated on his wooden crate of a throne; just the sad smell of damp earth. In the gloom, Paul's eyes assessed the strip of shabby carpet with its design of six interlocking rings; Slug's all-important clipboard, propped against one wall; du Toit's plastic helmet, lying in pride of place on the wooden crate. Kneeling, he picked the helmet up, causing the visor, which had been pushed upwards in order not to obscure the wearer's face, to come away in his hand and fall to the floor. All that had been holding it in place was a strip of brittle, yellowing sticky-tape.

He remembered Slug's warning: *Duck, hey, or you'll catch the support and the hut will collapse. It has happened.*

Fumblingly, he set the helmet and visor back on the throne, pressing the useless sticky-tape into place as he did so, then left again, carefully closing the door behind him. He didn't want the knob falling off as well!

Peering above the rim of the ditch, he saw that the rest of the club, Horton included, were advancing towards him around the edge of an otherwise empty field.

'Finally!' said du Toit on reaching the ditch. 'We've been looking everywhere!'

Was it Paul's imagination, or did Horton look particularly pleased to see him?

'Where else would I be?' he countered. 'Slug did tell me. I got the message.'

'You see!' cried Slug.

But du Toit just pushed ahead of them into the hut, Slug at his heels, and the door swung shut, leaving the others outside. Then Slug reappeared, clipboard at the ready, to sign them in.

'John Henry Labuschagne?'

'Present and correct.'

'Peter Angus Richard Kintock?'

'Present and correct.'

'Howard Strover?'

'Present and correct.'

'Timothy Hugh Horton?'

'Present and correct.'

'Paul Thomas Barnabas Harvey?'

Also present and correct, of course.

'Come on!' murmured Slug, nudging Paul through the door. 'We don't have all day.'

The captain, securely helmeted, was on his throne; the broken visor must have been tucked away somewhere, out of sight. Except Paul wasn't given time to ponder its whereabouts, since no sooner had they settled themselves at du Toit's feet than Slug began proclaiming the day's business. In particular, the fact that, far from being dressed down, Paul was to be promoted again following another successful task.

A revised order of precedence was read out: 'One: Murray. Two: Harvey. Three: Strover. Four: Horton. Five: Labuschagne. Six: Kintock.'

So! Paul was just behind Slug now. In this of all possible weeks. Or should that be impossible weeks? Almost number one. Within spitting distance.

'And before you start complaining again, Horton,' said du Toit, 'or you, hey, Strover, I want you both to demolish the hut next door. And it has to be done without the juniors seeing. Or even knowing. Okay? They must think it just fell down, *sommer so*. Like an act of God. Or the Bay of Pigs. Out of the blue. Understood?'

That evening, after supper, Paul found himself in need of the toilet before setting out for the day's watch. He chose the downstairs ones – they were closest – and it was here, on emerging from the stall, that he bumped into Slug, washing his hands at one of the basins.

'I didn't hear you come in,' he said suspiciously.

'I'm only washing my hands,' said Slug. 'Is it against the law for an *ou* to wash his hands?'

In the mirror that ran the length of the wall, the two of them regarded each other.

Then Slug came out with something like, 'It isn't always easy, hey, or tit, being his right-hand man. I thought it would be nicer. Anyway, soon it'll be your turn and ... '

But here he stopped, leaving unfinished whatever it was he'd been trying to say: building up perhaps to asking again if Paul could get him an invitation to the farm. Or was he wanting something less concrete? Friendship? Understanding? Protection? Now that Paul was on the up.

Paul could plainly see, in Slug's magnified pupils, a vast and desperate longing. The longing to be liked, to be other than what he was, no longer fat and wobbly, but slim and good-looking, just like du Toit. That and the beginning of tears, which was probably why he now turned away.

The week's events were having an effect on them all – and, as Paul followed Slug into the playground, he was trumped by some unexpected thoughts.

Why had he never seen how similar he was to Slug? Both of them outsiders. Both wanting to be other than how they were. To belong.

Which was what made them so vulnerable, of course, to du Toit.

When in fact they already did belong. Everyone did. For that had been another effect of the week: to bring Spier's much vaunted 'outside world' within – well, spitting distance.

And if no outside, then by default, no outsider either. Everyone was part of a greater whole. Willy-nilly, as his mother liked to say. All cohered. All were being held to account. No matter how insignificant or small (like the distant stars) they might imagine themselves to be.

He looked about him at the playground. The ochre earth, the line of equally red classrooms on the one side of it, the tuck shop at its centre, the white arch from which hung the school bell, the fields beyond. The compound where the masters lived, the compound for the servants, the ditch containing the club house. And sky, of course, the darkening sky. All cohering also. All linked.

It was, he told himself, against the natural order to keep forming clubs. Clubs just threw up barriers.

'Come on, Harvey!' he heard someone shout. 'Over here!' Lombard was waving at him from where he stood by the fence with Horton and Bentley major, thus encouraging Paul into an obliging run during which he also noticed that on the other side of the fence, parked more or less exactly where it had been the night before, was a recognisable car, its interior still lit by the glowing tips of two cigarettes.

It wasn't until the Saturday, though, that things came to a head, starting with the moment when Paul remembered to return the handkerchief Mosa had washed for him to its owner. He'd forgotten previously – not surprisingly, perhaps, given how the week had turned out – and it was only during that morning's Afrikaans lesson that thoughts of the handkerchief surfaced.

Afrikaans was the province of a part-time master called Marais, a youngish man, younger than almost all the other teachers, with the exception of Spier, though to link Marais and Spier was not an obvious thing to do. For, where Spier was slapdash and untidy, Marais always wore a perfectly pressed blue blazer, no matter how hot the weather, in the front pocket of which he kept two perfectly aligned gold pens. His trousers were always perfectly pressed, too, his dark hair precisely parted, his shoes vigorously polished. He looked less like a teacher, in point of fact, than a shop mannequin.

That morning, he was explaining the origin of certain Afrikaans terms. He did this by telling them about a group of religious refugees from France, known as the Huguenots. In 1685, during an earlier October – to the week, as it happened; the 22nd, to be precise, which Marais always was – Louis XIV of France had revoked something called the Edict of Nantes, by which the Huguenots had been guaranteed, as Protestants in a Catholic country, freedom of religious expression. Accordingly, they'd fled, some of them to the Cape.

On the blackboard, Marais wrote out a few names. His own to start with, followed by: *Franschoek*. Franschoek, he explained, had once been a 'French Corner'. Literally. Whilst many typically Afrikaans surnames also had unmistakably French origins.

Eight

François Villon = Viljoen
la Buscagne = Labuschagne
Le Clercq = de Klerk
du Toit

Another example of linkage, stretching across time in this case, not that Paul registered as much, since this was when he recalled the handkerchief. But then couldn't think where he'd put it. Until, just before the lesson's end, it came to him: in his locker, hidden under his tuck tin. Of course!

He resolved to collect it when changing after lunch to tidy up in the pavilion – those seniors not picked as spectators at the away game were instead always expected to make themselves useful about the school – during which time, either before or afterwards, he knew he'd almost certainly come across Pheko going about his own duties. And indeed, no sooner had Paul stepped on to the playing fields than there he was, the owner of the handkerchief, away in the distance, bent over his roller, making it a relatively easy matter for Paul to run over to him.

Coming to a sort of scarecrow attention in his tattered clothes, the young groundsman said, with a surprised smile, 'The *baas* looks better. No more blood. I am glad.'

'I've come to say thank you,' responded Paul, arrested by the force field of Pheko's smell. 'Mosa has washed your handkerchief for me.' He extracted it from his pocket. 'She ironed it also. I hope you'll be pleased. Here, take it!'

'The *baas* is very good,' said Pheko, releasing his grip on the roller in order to accept the proffered article. 'Your

161

Mosa also.' With his other hand, he'd started fumbling in his own pocket, from which he now produced a second handkerchief, not as white, and something else besides. Something Paul recognised from both Spier's and Mr du Toit's desks.

'Now Pheko has two handkerchiefs,' continued the groundsman, folding them together before returning them to his pocket. The comb-like object, meanwhile, remained in full view; and, as a pole-axed Paul started to turn away, it was raised by Pheko to his head, to prod at the tight curls there.

So! It *was* a comb he'd taken! A comb moreover belonging to Pheko, for what else could it mean if the groundsman now had the twin of it in his hand? A comb that would then end up in the hands of Mr du Toit, who did things for the government. Which was also where something further had ended up: Paul's report on seeing Pheko go with Spier into the master's bungalow.

During last week's exeat, Paul had thought (quite happily) that Spier should be stopped from talking politics to Pheko. And he hadn't really minded either his putative part in bringing this about. But, on seeing the duplicate comb, everything abruptly changed. Changed utterly. Of course, he still didn't know for sure what was happening. How could he? But he did realise he didn't want to be responsible for it. Whatever 'it' was. Not if he could possibly help it!

He also realised he must tell Spier. Tell him everything. He didn't know quite how he'd do this – in truth, he dreaded to think what the master might say in response

Eight

– but what other choice was there, in the final analysis? (Choice! How apt.) If he wanted to go on living with himself?

The baas *is very good*, Pheko had said. Well, only if he screwed up the courage to come clean with Spier about his duplicity.

First, though, he must head for the pavilion, since Botma, who was keeping an eye on how useful the stay-at-homes actually were, would undoubtedly want to check on him at some point. Then he found that, with his thoughts still centred on what he'd seen in Pheko's hand, it took him longer than usual to tidy things away. So that even when Botma did appear, there was still a mat or two in need of stowing.

'Come on, boy!' grunted the master, settling himself on a nearby piece of equipment in order to fiddle with and refill his smelly pipe. 'Do hurry up.'

'Yes, sir. Sorry, sir.' Whereafter he did at last manage to finish the afternoon's task to his and Botma's satisfaction.

'Right!' said Botma, looking up from his pipe. 'Off you go, then. I'll close up.'

'Yes, sir. Thank you, sir.'

Emerging with relief from the pavilion, Paul immediately started towards the masters' compound and his next task of the day – self-imposed this time. He hadn't gone far, however, before he was brought up short by a most extraordinary sight. First, he noticed two policemen standing by the gate that led into the compound; then, as he slowed, two more policemen appeared from inside the compound. In their wake:

Spier, his head lowered and wearing a jacket for once, dark blue, not unlike Marais's.

Another figure followed: Pheko, in his tattered khaki, arms held out before him, wrists handcuffed together, the metal of the handcuffs glinting in the sun. Then a further few policemen, their uniforms all matching the colour of Spier's jacket.

Why was it the clothing in particular that my younger self noticed? I can't really say. Unless it was because of a previous sighting, just as vivid, just as troubling, in which Spier had dispensed with clothes altogether.

I also like to imagine that Spier might have glanced upwards; that a look might have passed between the two of us. But what would the look have contained, if so? And anyway, I was too far away. The scene was another semi-distant tableau. Closer was Botma, who'd emerged from the pavilion himself by now, pipe in mouth, match at the ready. Although he didn't actually strike the match. Instead, like me, he just watched in stupefied silence as the police led Spier and the handcuffed Pheko away.

Nine

IT IS MORNING in Mokimolle and I am standing at the window of the dining room, drawn there by the dirge-like sound of a passing funeral procession. Up front, a coffin – top of the range, with brassy handles – lies across the shoulders of six suited mourners. Behind them stalks a cassocked priest. Then thirty or forty other mourners, many of them children and all so raggedly attired that, apart from their sighing song, you wouldn't think to connect them with the smartly dressed entourage at their head.

A soft wind is blowing. It lifts the eddying dust raised by the bare, metronomic feet of the mourners into an apparent veil that half obscures them as they turn a corner. Going, no doubt, in the direction of the cemetery – where I too am headed, once breakfast is over.

The houses on the street, each fronted by a stoep and, sometimes, a pavement tree for good measure, stand still and undisturbed, making me feel I may have dreamed the procession. No one appears to live in Mokimolle, that's the thing: the houses are just too quiet; and without the living, how then any dead?

But of course we do have the dead. I'm proof of that. I would never have come, were it not for past ghosts.

Quitting the window, I return with a wry smile to my unfinished breakfast. Soon, I tell myself – soon, Paul, soon! – the reckoning.

In 1962, Sunday has come round again: October 28th, which by evening would mark the end of the Cuban missile crisis, since it was then that Khrushchev broadcast his agreement to dismantle his missile sites in return for America promising to stop the blockade, not invade Cuba and, at the same time, withdraw its own missiles from Turkey. Although this last detail would only emerge much later.

In Pretoria, that morning, Paul was climbing with a heavy heart into the back of a dusty truck.

'Everything all right?' queried Mr du Toit, twisting round to get a better look at his sombre expression. 'You haven't been frightened, have you, by what's been happening? 'Cause it isn't necessary, hey. Like I've just been telling Laura, you're quite safe here. Honestly. We all are. Believe me.'

Words which, coiled about as they were with the smoke that also issued from his mouth, might have had a more calming effect had Paul been able to think they encompassed not just Cuba, but Spier's arrest as well. Although it wasn't absolutely certain of course that Spier had been arrested. All Paul had to go on, in the absence of anyone confirming anything, was what he'd seen. Maybe it was just the handcuffed Pheko who'd been taken into custody? For stealing perhaps – blacks often stole; you were always hearing stories. In which case, Spier might have been present purely as a witness, or as a spokesman for Pheko, who couldn't be expected to defend or speak for himself. Blacks didn't have the confidence; the language; the right.

Though on the other hand, Paul hadn't seen Spier at all on Saturday evening, which often you did. And there was this to consider too: Botma's freighted words in the wake of the startling scene they'd both witnessed.

'I think it's best,' he'd said, lighting his pipe finally, 'if you don't say anything to anyone, Harvey, about what we've just seen. Okay? For the time being. You don't want to start a nasty rumour.'

So all through supper, a particularly anxious sunset watch, getting ready for bed, even after lights-out as he lay staring again at the stars, Paul hadn't uttered a word. Just worried and wondered, wondered and worried. Alone in his misery.

'But where is Andre?' Mr du Toit was asking. 'Why does he always, but always keep us waiting?'

'Because he's a hopeless slowcoach, Pa,' said Laura. 'You ought to teach him a lesson.'

'How?'

'Stop his pocket money or something.'

'It's a thought. But here he comes. *Uiteindelik*! Good of you to grace us with your presence.' This as du Toit clambered into the back of the truck alongside Paul. 'What's your excuse this time?' The key was turned in the ignition. 'It had better be good.' The engine chuntered into life.

'So, Pa, tell us,' was du Toit's impervious response, 'this Castro and the Soviet missiles, you must have heard. We've been talking about it all week, hey, Harvey? What does the government think?'

The truck was turning into the street to begin its farmward journey. First past the houses that stood so proud in their well-tended gardens. Then the newer, less affluent suburbs on the edge of town: smaller houses, meaner gardens. Then a dirt road, dust behind them, parched earth to either side and, at moments, waddling women with huge boxes on their heads in the middle distance, since that was how black people always carried their possessions: on their heads, in boxes, standing proud. Not proud like the houses that surrounded St Luke's, but still, in their own way, proud.

In the meantime, the first of that day's conversations was continuing thus:

'Like I've just told Laura,' Mr du Toit was saying, 'and Paul. You're safe here. We all are. No need to worry.'

'Is it serious, though?'

'*Ja*, of course it's serious. You've heard me talk about how dangerous these commies are.'

'So we should be worrying, then!'

'What you must worry about,' interjected Laura, 'is if Pa stops your pocket money.'

'Why would he do that?'

'For being such a slowcoach, of course. Hey, Pa?'

'That wasn't my fault,' said du Toit. 'Blame Stanford. I had to find Matron for some stupid meeting they're supposed to be having, all the staff.'

'A staff meeting?' asked Mr du Toit sharply. 'On a Sunday? Really?'

'So you can't blame me,' continued Paul's back-seat companion, shooting him the sort of look – a look of exasperated complicity, one that assumed the two of them to be equal in their outrage at the way boys could be treated – which previously he would have prized. But not today. Today he just looked quickly away, through the dusty window, to concentrate instead on Pretoria's newer, less affluent suburbs; then the veld, quite unaffluent.

At the wheel, Mr du Toit, having allowed the blame for his son's tardiness to remain at Stanford's door, was asking about their respective weeks; about some concert Laura was practising for; and had anything else happened? Of note. Apart from Cuba. That they wanted to tell him about.

Well?

Mercifully, the questions stopped at this point, since by now they'd reached the farm. Mr du Toit parked, as before, under a blue gum, and together they trooped on to the stoep to find that Violet had again set out some rusks and cooldrink for them. Laura vanished with hers along the stoep, while Mr du Toit, hovering for a moment, lit yet another cigarette from the packet he always kept in his shirt pocket and said, 'The old boy's still feeling *'n bietjie vrot*, I'm afraid. So! No arguments today. All right? I haven't the patience and you know what it means to him.' Casually, he ruffled the Brylcreemed smoothness of his son's blond hair.

'Okay, Pa, okay,' said du Toit, squirming. 'I get the message.'

'You don't mind, Paul, do you?' continued Mr du Toit, cat-like eyes swivelling in his direction.

'Of course not, sir,' said Paul.

'Sir!' echoed Mr du Toit with a chuckle. 'I like it! Sir!'

Then he also vanished, still chuckling, into the house and there was no one to overhear Paul say, as they took up their cooldrinks, 'So now you have to tell me – you just have to!'

'Tell you what?'

'The police were there yesterday, you know. Maybe they'd even been there before, watching from a car. I saw something, that's for sure. Anyway, Pheko was in handcuffs and Spier was with him and ... '

'Spier?' repeated du Toit. 'You mean it's happened at last!'

'What, though?' persisted Paul. 'What's happened?' And here it slipped out – 'Andre!' – the only time (I think) he ever called du Toit by his Christian name. 'It isn't fair, keeping me in the dark like this.'

He tried to encourage a fuller response by listing the connections he could already make himself. In no special order, these were:

Is this about keeping the country safe?

Nine

Die rooi gevaar.

And/or the *swart* one.

The comb. His report.

Ending with another: 'You have to tell me! Please!'

He'd started the list while they were both still standing on the stoep; by its close, they were almost at the *koppie* that overlooked the foul-smelling dam and, beyond it, Tsebo's *kraal*.

It was here, litany finished, that du Toit said, 'Remember when you got so mad about your stupid diary?'

'Of course I do.'

'Because I'd seen something you didn't want anyone else to know about. Like some of the things you wrote about me, which weren't very nice, hey, you must admit; also when your grandmother said she thought this country wasn't safe any more, how you ought to go and live with her in England. Crazy stuff like that. Which even *you* didn't like because you also said – I saw that too – how you felt about being such a *sout-piel*. So then I had my brainwave!'

'Brainwave?'

'I asked you to join my club, duh! A bit because I pitied you, like with Slug. Only with Slug, it's how fat he is. But also – it's true – I knew you could help me with Pa. You don't know what it's like, how he always goes on at me to do things better, be a *ware* du Toit. You've seen the photos.'

'You mean … ?'

'*Ja*, on the walls. Pa's always telling me how hard they worked to make a place for us. Which Pa does too, but in a different way: he also wants South Africa to shine. *And* me – because now I'm growing up, he says, now I must also do the same. Be like them. Him. Then he found out that your parents know that priest whose son was put under house arrest last week, the one who also knows Spier – that's the only reason, hey, why Pa asked you all to visit – anyhow, that's also when I had my brainwave. I thought that if *we* did some spying, just the two of us, because you're good at noticing things, but I've already told you that, then I could share with Pa what we saw or found. And if what you say is right – about Spier, I mean, but I'll ask him before lunch, he can tell us then – well, it's worked, hey. It's really, really worked and he can't accuse me any more of only being Ma's son.'

As with other such moments from that pivotal month, I can't swear those were his exact words. Though, as when he'd first asked me, also on the farm, to watch and take note, that was certainly the gist of it. The underlying thrust.

'But right now,' he said in conclusion, 'we've got Tsebo to visit. Last one there is a *vrot* tomato!' Adding, once they'd both arrived, panting, at the bamboo fence surrounding the *kraal*, 'Remember! We don't go into the hut unless he asks. And leave the talking to me, okay?'

They found the old man in much the same spot and posture as a fortnight ago: stick to hand, on a chair in the sun.

'*Dumela*,' murmured du Toit, coming to a standstill.

'*Dumela*, Andre. *Dumela*, Harvey,' replied Tsebo, favouring each of them with a distinct smile. 'It is nice to see you again. Violet is cooking a special lunch. Much better than school, she says. What do you eat most, Harvey?'

Paul would have quite liked to specify – it was a novelty for him, to be standing in a *kraal*, conversing with a black man – but du Toit prevented this by asking Tsebo how he'd been feeling. And then, after the old man had explained that he wasn't so well this week, by just as quickly posing a string of further questions, some of them quite unnecessary-sounding. As though he feared even the slightest of interventions from Paul. Why?

Then another thought: although, for Paul, black people (even Mosa) were always confined to the sidelines, much like the chorus in a Greek play (they'd studied one last term), here was du Toit talking directly to Tsebo in a manner that put him in mind of Pheko handing him the handkerchief. Pheko, who'd afterwards been led away in handcuffs.

Meanwhile, du Toit, having asked the last of his questions, was stepping backwards and Tsebo was enquiring softly, 'Do you see your mother next week?'

Tightly, du Toit nodded.

'I have a parcel for her, please. She gave this book to Tsebo a long time ago. Can you take it back?'

Again du Toit nodded.

'It is in the hut. On the table.'

While du Toit went in search of the parcel, the old man, looking hard at Paul, said, 'It makes me very happy that you are here again. A friend for Andre is good.' Then, as du Toit emerged from the hut with a small, roughly wrapped parcel under one arm, he raised a hand in farewell. 'Be safe! And come back soon.'

Du Toit took the lead again on quitting the *kraal*, with Paul allowing a certain distance to develop between them as he digested their encounter with Tsebo. Until at last, having decided he had nothing to lose, he came up close to ask of the back of du Toit's suntanned neck, 'Where do you go, to see your mother?'

The muscles in du Toit's neck tightened. But that was all. No slackening of pace. No turning around.

'Lombard says…' persevered Paul.

Now du Toit did swing round, staring him down with those icy blue eyes of his.

'Lombard,' he spat, 'knows nothing. Lombard doesn't even know how to mind his own beeswax. And that's what Ma is – okay? Mine and no one else's. Not even Laura's. Got that?'

On regaining the house, which, after this exchange, they did in virtual silence, du Toit left Paul alone for a bit while he went (or so he said) to talk to his father. Then they repaired to du Toit's room, where somehow they managed to distract themselves, du Toit with his Dinky toys, Paul by immersing himself once more in du Toit's comics, until it was time to revisit the gloomy dining room with its dark, old-fashioned furnishings and all those photographic portraits on the wall.

'I hope the *baas* is hungry?' Violet said to Paul as she set down her dishes on the table. 'It's *tamatiebredie*, from the madam's old recipe. Rice also, and a pudding for later, very big, Violet's best.'

'Thank you, Violet,' said Mr du Toit, before lowering his head, closing his eyes and going on to murmur, 'O *Here, en U gee aan hulle almal spyse op die regte tyd. U voed uit U milde hand en vervul alles wat op aarde leef met U ryke seën. Amen.'*

Once everyone had helped themselves, and after advising Laura that she could learn too, if she listened, he then launched into a favoured subject of Spier's: the Western world and communism. He explained how, as an ideology, communism wanted (just as President Kennedy had said) world domination. South Africa, therefore, had a vital role to play in the fight to keep the Western world free from all this. But – and it was a big but – there were elements within the country who wanted otherwise. Who believed in communism, actually held by it, even followed its precepts. If you could credit such a thing!

At first, manifestations of this attitude had been relatively mild, he said. Ill-considered talk, union activity, strikes; stuff like that. Recently, however, things had escalated. Sabotage of important buildings, for instance, and now an article in that morning's *Sunday Times* about a hitherto secret branch of the banned African National Congress called *Umkonto we Sizwe*, or 'Spear of the Nation', which had sent the paper a 'proclamation' announcing that from now on its motto would be 'a life for a life' in its campaign to overthrow 'white rule in South Africa'. Quotes from the article were indicated by the movement, in mid-air, of paired fingers doing duty as quotation marks.

Which was why, Mr du Toit said, the government had needed to come up with something like house arrest.

'And so, boys, we get to our friend Simon Tindall. Simon Tindall and *his* friend, Andrew Spier.'

Without going into specifics – he said he couldn't do that, it was better kept secret how he did things – he nonetheless told them that, as a concerned citizen of the best country in the world, he must always do his utmost to protect the government from people like Simon Tindall. People who were potentially dangerous in what they said; what they thought. So, when he had learned that Peggy and Douglas knew Simon's father, he'd grabbed the opportunity to find out more. This didn't mean he hadn't wanted to meet Peggy and Douglas too; of course he had. They seemed delightful and anyway, he liked showing newcomers the ropes.

At the same time, he'd learned – at cricket maybe? he couldn't now remember – that Simon Tindall knew Andrew Spier, which was what had given him the idea that someone should start keeping an eye on Spier as well. Because he'd already heard from Andre of course all about this General Knowledge Club and the sorts of things that were discussed there. Disgraceful, really.

Then the pair of them – here Mr du Toit's green eyes darted approvingly from du Toit to Paul and back again – had established a link between Spier and the school groundsman. Which the authorities had taken most seriously. When told. As well they might. For Spier was clearly spreading dissent not only among his own pupils, bad enough, but the servants too. Imagine!

Spier and the groundsman would now be questioned, he said, and, if what everyone suspected was true, put on trial, just like that other troublemaker Mr Mandela, then sent away for a very long time. Years and years and years, with any luck.

'You boys can be very proud,' he concluded, 'of what you've helped us to achieve. You're quite a team.' He raised his beer. 'Shall we toast ourselves? Why not? I think we deserve it.'

If Paul's stomach had been knotted at the start of the meal, by the time Violet's pudding was finished it had practically turned to stone. Except that he didn't, in reality, pay much attention to his body's response to Mr du Toit's long lecture. He'd gone into mild shock, I suppose, and moved through the rest of the exeat in something of a daze.

After lunch, as Violet smilingly cleared away the plates, Mr du Toit took the coffee she'd brought him to his study. He wanted, he told them, to finish the paper. Meanwhile, they were to amuse themselves, please, and not make too much noise. It was a Sunday, remember: the day of the Lord; one of rest.

(Only later would this make me smile: that he could mouth such a platitude when he himself actually never stopped working; for what else had my parents' own

Sunday visit been, if not work? A labour, indeed, of love.
Another irony.)

Laura vanished too, leaving du Toit to say, with a
smirk, 'Happy now?'

'Happy?'

'I don't know about you, but *I'm* going to my room.'

Paul could, he supposed, have gone with him,
although he didn't see that du Toit's comics – or even the
Dinky toys – would distract him now. Nor did he fancy
being in du Toit's company much. So he stepped outside
rather, into the afternoon heat.

Initially, he just wandered about in front of the house,
kicking at loose stones. Then, because it was too hot
in the sun and he worried that he might be seen from
Mr du Toit's study, he headed for the nearest of the
outbuildings, the one containing the old car on bricks and
the agricultural machinery.

It was here, on the seat of a rusted tractor, as he fiddled
restlessly with the gearstick, that Laura found him.

'Violet noticed,' she explained. 'That you'd been left
on your own. Have you two argued?'

'No.'

'*Yissus*, but he's rude, my *boet*. He's lucky to have
friends.'

At lunch, she'd been in the same simple dress she'd
worn on his first visit, blue like her eyes; since lunch,
however, she'd changed into shorts and a T-shirt, clothing
which allowed her to clamber easily on to the nose of
the tractor, where she now settled. 'Last time,' she said,
'you started to tell me about this club of his. Remember?

Nine

I suppose Lombard must have been a member too, until he made the mistake of talking to Andre about Ma. Tell me again, how does it work exactly?'

Paul hadn't imagined the exeat providing him with another chance to find out about du Toit's mother and Lombard. Yet here it was, all of a sudden, in the shape of the unapproachable Laura, unapproachable no longer.

So, in defiance of what du Toit had once told him – *If you want to stay in the club, you mustn't talk about it to other people. Not ever. Got that?* – he explained precisely how it worked. Then, while she was digesting this information, he snuck in his own question about Lombard and Mrs du Toit.

Frowning – she obviously didn't think much of how her brother's club was ordered – she said, 'Hell, that's pathetic, treating your own friends in that way. If Ma knew ... '

Their mother, it now came out, was from Johannesburg originally. English-speaking and a gifted musician, she played both the piano and the violin, instruments she also taught at a school in Johannesburg, since that was where she'd gone, back home, after she and Mr du Toit had separated.

'They're not divorced – Pa won't allow a divorce; it's against God's law, he says – but she's not coming back, it just wouldn't work. Although she still has things here, instruments and stuff, which he won't allow her to take away.'

Why wouldn't it work, the marriage? Well, they were very different, apparently. Not only was she English-speaking – which was why, incidentally, Laura and Andre had been sent to English-speaking schools, against the wishes of her father, but her mother had insisted – she was also more of a city person and quite different politically, too. For example, whatever it was that Mr du Toit did for the government, Mrs du Toit hadn't approved. In fact, it was a mystery really, why they'd got together in the first place, though both of them had often told her how they'd met at a concert in Pretoria where Mrs du Toit was playing and how Mr du Toit had gone up afterwards to congratulate her on her technique. It had, he said, been like hearing angels. Or something soppy like that.

Her mother was also very pretty. That was a factor too. Everyone said how beautiful she was. Soft and kind. Not at all like her hard father.

Another difference.

'I have more of Ma in me than Andre does,' she said, still frowning. 'But that doesn't mean he doesn't hate her being gone. It's why he's like he is, really. *Pak vol* anger, which he doesn't know what to do with, that's what Violet says. She's sort of our mother now. Here, I mean, at home. Not when we visit Jo'burg, obviously. She's known us since we were babies. Tsebo also. They take care of us. Or try to.'

'And Lombard?' asked Paul. 'What happened for him and your ... ' he hesitated slightly before deploying the Afrikaans word ' ... *boet* to argue?'

It turned out that Laura, who'd liked Lombard – in fact her *boet* used to tease her that she really *smaaked* him, which was silly, she didn't, he was too young for her, but anyway – one time she'd had much the same conversation with Lombard as she was having now with Paul, about their mother and things. But then Lombard had made the mistake of telling Andre he understood, which Andre hadn't liked because after that Lombard hadn't been asked back. No one had. Until now.

'So be warned!' she said. 'If you want to stay in this mad club of his, you'd better keep your trap shut. And now you have to tell *me* something! What Pa said at lunch. All that stuff about politics and everything and that silly master of yours, who's been arrested. I don't understand why Pa had to thank you.'

Did I explain? Or was this a confidence too far? I don't honestly remember. All I can be certain of is that this was pretty much the moment when I decided, once and for all, that I no longer wished to be a member of du Toit's 'mad' club.

First, though, there was the rest of the exeat to endure. Laura stayed with me for some of it; I think we might even have gone walking together about the farm. Then it was time for more cooldrink on the stoep and the drive back to school, stopping at St Mary's on the way to deposit Laura, who said cheerily as she got out of the truck, 'See you later, alligators!'

Though she never would, of course. Not in my case, anyway.

Then St Luke's and the surprise sight of my parents standing on the steps alongside Stanford in a pose that called to mind the statues you often find in the Transvaal of rifled men and bonneted women, *Voortrekkers*, facing up to their future with bronzed resolve.

'Is that your parents, there on the steps?' said Mr du Toit, bringing the truck to a halt. 'Something wrong, do you think?'

In fact, something was right. My parents, guessing that I might have found the week upsetting, had come to check I was okay, even though they could only stay a moment.

'Mum! Dad!' I remember running up to them at speed and how my mother scooped me into her arms, holding me tight, while my father, standing slightly to one side, contented himself with just a pat on the head.

'We wanted to make sure you were all right,' she said. 'With all that's been going on. We didn't like to think of you worrying.'

She couldn't have known this then, but, by coincidence, she must have been speaking at around the time Khrushchev was making his broadcast.

'Yes,' interrupted Stanford with, for him, an uncharacteristic, if rueful, smile. 'What a week, hey, one way and another? Bound to get quite a write-up in the history books.'

'As long as you've not been fretting unduly,' said my mother. 'That's the main thing. Now! Have you said goodbye to Mr du Toit? And thanked him properly for having you? How *was* your day? Fun?'

'I certainly hope so!' said a deep voice.

We'd been joined by both du Toits, the one shadowing the other.

Nine

'Nice to see you, Peggy. Douglas.' Du Toit senior nodded at each of my parents in turn. 'Everything all right?'

'Now it is,' said Douglas. 'Thank you very much.'

'It's only,' added Peggy, 'that because of last week, well, you know, we just felt we ought to check that Paul hadn't been worrying.'

'*Ag*,' said Mr du Toit, 'we talked it through at lunch. Didn't we, boys? They realise there's nothing to be concerned about. Not here. Not now.'

'Good,' said Peggy. 'I'm glad. That's what we want to hear. Isn't it, dear?' She slipped her hand into my father's. 'But come! We'd better get going. Exeat's over.'

The memory of my parents standing hand in hand on the school steps has brought sudden tears to my eyes. Unwanted too because, if I am to do today what I have come to Mokimolle to do, I mustn't be distracted. It's time to move on.

Downing the last of my coffee, I push back my chair and make for the hallway, where I encounter Giles in another of his shirts, this one covered in what look like splotches of paint, splashed there in a design frenzy.

'On your way, then?' he asks.

I nod.

'You can always leave your stuff here, you know – ' he gestures towards the bag in my hand ' – if you do want to explore a bit first. Safer than in the car.'

I thank him, but say I really must be off.

'Where next? The Kruger? Or aren't you into wildlife?'

I just shrug.

'Personally,' he says, 'if I go east, it's to the coast. Though you have to be careful, hey, of the currents. Not to mention the sharks!'

He's already written out my bill, which he now presents. I settle up and ask him please to compliment Lawrence again on his food. 'Including breakfast.'

'Well, you must just come back, then,' replies Giles. 'Now you know what a fantastic country this is.' He smiles. 'Well, in parts.' He opens the front door. 'Travel safely!'

As I drive slowly through the small town, I relive my final moments with du Toit, which takes me back again to the playground, where my younger self is hunting for him. It's some time during the following week, after we've been told that the world is not to end.

Except that I couldn't find him, not at first. Then I saw Slug, who suggested the club house.

Approaching it, as one had to, via the edge of the playing field, I thought of Pheko, Pheko and Spier, which stiffened my resolve. I summoned Sydney Carton. *It is a far, far better thing that I do than I have ever done.* Then a formulation of my mother's: *sticks and stones may break your bones, but words will never hurt you.* And Laura's: *pathetic, treating your own friends in that way…*

Not forgetting Mr du Toit's prophecy that Spier and the groundsman would be sent away for *years and years and years, with any luck.*

The most potent rallying cry of them all.

Nine

I found him on his own, sitting hunched on his throne, his plastic helmet in his lap, a roll of fresh Sellotape in one hand. The door was open; he hadn't bothered to shut it, perhaps because he needed light in order to see what he was doing. So I was able to observe him for some minutes without knocking. And could also start speaking without having to ask permission first.

I told him that I was leaving his club. I borrowed Laura's phrase. I told him it – he – was pathetic. Let someone else aspire to being his right-hand man if they wanted to. Nor was I scared of him any more, I continued, using my mother's phrase. *Sticks and stones.* He could call me anything he liked. I'd rather not belong at all, I said, than be in a club like his. Adding that when I got back to the playground, I was going to tell Slug what I'd done. 'If Slug has any sense,' I threw in for good measure, 'he will do the same. I've seen how he looks at you.'

Then I turned away, leaving him there, helmet still unfixed. And, as I pushed roughly past the juniors who had emerged from their own hut to see who'd been berating du Toit, I silently recited one last exhortation to myself:

If you can bear to hear the truth you've spoken
Twisted by knaves to make a trap for fools,
Or watch the things you gave your life to, broken,
And stoop and build 'em up with worn-out tools …

I have reached the outskirts of the town, the last of its sparse bungalows, where I come across a sign that reads:

CEMETERY ¼ MILE. No turning back now. Somewhat apprehensively, I nose the car along a road that soon turns from tar to bumpy dirt and dust.

As I do this, the past makes proper space at last for the present: my pilgrimage.

I'm a man in my sixties, near the end of his professional life. But not there yet, thanks to which – and the nature of my work – I'm also easy to track down. The articles I write as a political journalist about what the West is pleased to call the developing world (or sometimes, the third world) can be readily accessed on the net, often with an email address attached. And it was to this address that Pheko had written, having lifted it from an article of mine about Nigeria's criminalisation of same-sex relations, a particular bugbear for me, as a gay man.

He thought perhaps I mightn't remember him, so he began by explaining that, once upon a time, he'd been a groundsman at my old school, St Luke's. Had once lent me, even, his handkerchief, which I'd kindly had laundered before returning it. Though that was not a thing I'd likely recall. Such an unimportant detail. He went on to say that he and his partner had often read my articles, always with gratitude and appreciation that someone living in the UK should write about stuff like homosexuality in Nigeria; or how fine the South African constitution was, something else I've been known to cover, especially in relation to the creeping corruption that present-day South Africa is heir to. Writings such as mine, he said, were important: they held people to account.

Nine

I wasn't sure I agreed with him; what I do has always felt piffling to me, of quite little account, in the final analysis. And started far too late, of course. Though I do try to write about things that need addressing.

But that's by the by; it's what he said next that mattered. His partner, he informed me, was someone I would most surely remember. I had, after all, been a favourite of his.

Andrew Spier. My old history master.

Then it all came pouring out. In 1962, he and Andrew, he wrote, had been arrested on suspicion of political activity; and in the course of being questioned, when Andrew had been asked if there was anything else to their meetings – somehow the authorities had learned that he used to visit Andrew in his bungalow – Andrew, because he was that sort of man, having at first tried to protect Pheko, had then, once he'd seen what was coming, what was inevitable, not even hesitated. Others would have; most did, in similar circumstances. But Andrew was exceptional. Yes, he'd said, no question. No question at all. He and Pheko were lovers. They stood as one.

This bombshell meant, of course, that they were charged not only for having inter-racial sex under the so-called Immorality Act, but for sodomy too, equally illegal, and imprisoned for an initial period of five years. Though all in all they'd actually served just over twenty, since, as a result also of their behaviour in prison and things that were said there to and by other prisoners, further charges, this time related to treason, were brought against them the moment their initial stretch had ended.

North Facing

They were finally released, Andrew first, Pheko some years later, in the mid-eighties, whereupon Andrew, who'd inherited some money from his parents, long since dead, bought a smallholding in the vicinity of a place now called Mokimolle, where Pheko had come to live as well, ostensibly as Andrew's servant. By this stage South Africa had bigger fish to fry, so, although the local police did keep an eye on them, sort of, they weren't harassed. Then came the release of Mandela, elections, the new South Africa, a rainbow nation. Under the country's redrawn constitution, they'd even been able to marry. The last twenty years or so had, in consequence, been most contented. They didn't have much money, wrote Pheko, but they could grow their own vegetables, they had a cow, they were happy. They didn't go out and about much; they kept themselves to themselves. But that was how they liked it. To have each other. It was all they'd ever wanted, really. Just to be together.

Then Andrew had developed cancer. And now Pheko had learned that he, too, was quite ill. Which was why he was writing. Before his own death, he said, he must do what he and Andrew had so often talked about doing, but never had: write to say that they remembered me and to thank me for my journalism.

Up ahead, the road turns and I see the cemetery: a wire fence, a metal gate, then maybe five acres of graves. I park the car and approach the gate. The graves nearest the fence all have headstones, either of granite or marble – stone, anyway – while those farthest from it are simple crosses of wood.

Nine

Where will the grave I'm seeking be located? I wonder. Or will there be two? My frantic correspondence with the town clerk after my initial emails to Pheko had gone unanswered had filled in certain of the gaps; but it hadn't supplied every detail. Not by a long chalk.

I notice the funeral procession from earlier, clustered around a freshly dug grave at the far end of the cemetery. A few of the more tattily dressed mourners are in the process of shovelling earth into the grave, while the priest (job done, presumably) is walking in my direction, speaking into a mobile phone.

I wait until he emerges through the gate, then step forward. He finishes his call and says, with a pleasant smile, 'May I help?'

Against the prevailing blackness of cassock and skin, his teeth are dazzling.

'I'm looking for a grave,' I say.

'Whose?'

'Well, two graves, actually. Andrew Spier's, and one for Pheko Tswana.'

'You knew them?' He sounds more delighted than surprised, as though it is entirely natural that a complete stranger should come to this isolated cemetery in search of their final resting place.

'A little. Long ago.'

He frowns. 'Ah, the bad old days.'

Not words to welcome, true though they are.

'In recent times,' he continues, seeming not to notice how his remark has affected me, 'their lives were quite different. Happily. They were a sort of inspiration, in fact, the way they lived together. I was honoured to be their priest.' The frown becomes another dazzling smile. 'Not that either of them had much time for religion! I had to be very careful not to talk about God when I visited. But still, they were good men. As I say, an inspiration. A true inspiration.'

'For me too,' I say, managing to speak at last.

'How did you know them?'

He has started back through the gate and, as we walk towards the centre of the cemetery, I offer him a little of my background. Just the barest outline. That I'd been a pupil of Spier's for a while, until – in the November of 1962 – my English grandmother had died and my mother, having returned to England to close up her house, had all at once decided that she wanted to stay there. In her childhood home. Meaning that, at the end of that same year, I'd left my school and flown with my father to England, where I'd lived ever since.

'So I suppose,' muses the priest, 'you don't really think of yourself as South African any more. Even though you were born here. Just a visitor these days. Is that correct? Still, you've come a very long way, after a very long time, to visit. That says something. He must have meant a great deal to you, your old teacher.'

We've reached that part of the cemetery where headstones give way to wooden crosses. Up ahead, the mourners from the finished funeral are gradually dispersing, the children by running.

'Here we are! This is them.' He steps back. 'And please, if you need anything more, just ring.'

Nine

He extends the hand with which he's been gesturing to shake my own, then presses into it a card with his phone number on it, plus the details of his church and a small picture.

'Be safe. Go well.'

He rejoins the mourners, the running children, heading with them for the gate.

Left alone, I remain for a fraction longer with the memory of our move to England. Of how, in this quite unexpected of ways, my grandmother had finally got what she'd always wanted: a safe exit for us from South Africa. Although no one ever talked about any of this afterwards. What my father had felt about following my mother back to where they'd started, he never said. Just as he stopped talking also, in later years, about how he'd dreamed once of being an engineer. Instead, he simply shut himself away in his workshop, surrounded by objects which, ironically, he still appeared loath to let go of, he who'd relinquished so much else.

My mother, too, kept largely silent; if she ever referred to South Africa, it was in the most general and innocuous of terms. Those blue, blue skies (how she'd used to long for a cloud, she would say); the dryness of the veld; the pitiful lack of culture, plays and concerts and the like. Nothing about servants ever; or politics; or the Afrikaners; or knowing a man by the name of du Toit – her part in all of that. The only man in her life, she would tell people – well, when he wasn't in his wretched workshop – was Douglas. Who, if he were present, would nod agreeably. *For me too*, he would say. *Aren't I lucky to have her?*

Thus did my parents turn their backs on South Africa;
and for the longest of whiles I did the same, happy like
them to forget all about du Toit and fellow-sufferers like
Slug, whom I never did talk to in the playground, as I'd
promised myself I would. Though I still wonder – but
only with Slug, never du Toit; he and his ilk can take care
of themselves – what became of him. Did he perhaps
lose weight as he grew up, emerging from childhood's
chrysalis into a happier, sleeker adulthood, where he was
seldom, if ever, teased? It comforts me to think this.

And so it all continued until, eventually, come my
early forties – yes, that late! – after the unexpected deaths
of both my mother and my father, I was helped from my
own chrysalis by a miracle man called Josh, who, among
the many things he did for me, urged me to revisit, on
my own terms, what had happened in childhood and
bit by bit make sense of it. To include South Africa in
the countries I wrote about. Partly in expiation, but also
in an effort to understand my past. Why my parents
had done what they had. Why *I* had. Things like my
father telling me once, *Adults can be fallible. Remember
that and you won't go far wrong in life.* Or how my
mother could later say, which I remember her doing on
more than one occasion, as she looked about her at my
grandmother's glorious garden, now ours: 'South-facing.
As it should be.'

It's where I live still, my grandmother's house, having
first shared it with Josh, with whom I shared all things
until he stupidly stepped one day in front of a car. Two
long, hard years ago. Which is why I have come to make

amends – insofar as amends can be made, of course – on my own.

Turning from my memories, I finally confront the double headstone before me, veld-coloured and quite weathered-looking already, despite its newness. The left-hand stone reads: Andrew Gordon Spier, 1939–2015. The right-hand one: Pheko Tswana, 1942–2016.

Underneath, traversing both gravestones and therefore linking them, is a sentence which, because of my tears, I at first imagine I will have some difficulty deciphering. But actually don't. I know the sentence by heart, you see. It comes from a favourite novel, first encountered, thanks to Josh, in the library where we also met; one in a long line of such libraries that stretch for me all the way from St Luke's to the present, providers of reading and refuge and light.

The sentence runs:

So we beat on, boats against the current, borne back ceaselessly into the past.

Acknowledgements

Thanks to: My inestimable agent, Laura Morris; Candida Lacey and all of team Myriad, most especially Emma Dowson, Linda McQueen and Dawn Sackett; Alistair Beaton, Halton Cheadle, Damon Galgut, Paul Herzberg, Jennifer Kavanagh, Allan Leas, Jack Lewis, Gaby Naher, Neil Olson, Kathleen Satchwell, Wendy Searle, Edmund White; and of course Peter, whose support and love has been the most vital help of all.

The extract from *The Song Before it is Sung* (Bloomsbury 2008) is quoted by kind permission of Justin Cartwright.

The line from 'Elsewhere' in *Citizen of Elsewhere* (Happenstance 2013) is quoted by kind permission of Jonty Driver.

MORE FROM MYRIAD

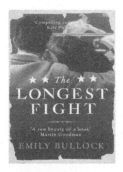

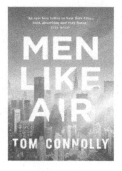

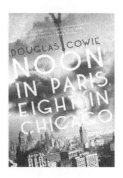

MORE FROM MYRIAD

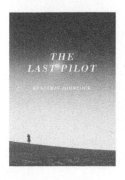

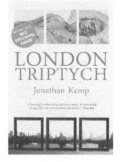

MORE FROM MYRIAD

Sign up to our mailing list at
www.myriadeditions.com
Follow us on Facebook and Twitter

Tony Peake was born in South Africa but has lived most of his life in the UK. He is an acclaimed short story writer with work in many anthologies including *The Penguin Book of Contemporary South African Short Stories*, *The Mammoth Book of Gay Short Stories* and *Best British Short Stories 2016*. He is the author of two novels, *A Summer Tide* (1993) and *Son to the Father* (1995), and of *Derek Jarman: A Biography* (1999).